donation
12/08

BLACK DIAMONDS

by

Barry Bonner

authorHOUSE®

AuthorHouse™
1663 Liberty Drive, Suite 200
Bloomington, IN 47403
www.authorhouse.com
Phone: 1-800-839-8640

First published by AuthorHouse 5/28/2008

ISBN: 978-1-4343-7667-1 (sc)

Library of Congress Control Number: 2008902935

Printed in the United States of America
Bloomington, Indiana

This book is printed on acid-free paper.

THIS ONE'S FOR
JACK
THEO
BEALL
WHO FOUGHT THE GOOD FIGHT

CHAPTER 1

Wapakonetka County, Ohio lies to the south, not far from West Virginia and Kentucky. The Rampart Mountain Range hems in a sprawling, rolling countryside stretching mile after mile north to south as far as you can see. A checkerboard of colors created by the many small farms with their fields of tomatoes, corn, and sugar beets shine like sheets of satin under the white, life-giving sun. Thick pine forests descend from the mountain peaks like the towering masts of sailing ships, crowding along the sides of steep ravines, wet with the sparkling, ice-cold water of tiny streams. The pines finally give way to scattered clusters of oaks, maples and hickory trees lower down, their large forests having been cut down long ago to make way for the farmers. To see the valley just at sunrise with the night mist fading in the warmth of daylight is to feel the silent, peaceful landscape surrounding you—a sense of a paradise of sorts.

The wind blows gently and the birds begin to sing their chorus of joy and thanksgiving—a celebration, as the sun, perfectly round, glows orange and bronze like a fiery furnace. But all this is a deceiving façade. The further south you travel there comes a feeling of loneliness, deadness—stretching far in all directions. Quite suddenly the earth is gloomy and forbidding even beneath the brilliant, silky blue sky. The fertile, rolling fields, rising and falling, flow into poisoned ground. The trees and vegetation are stunted, dry and parched. Oasis' of fiddle ferns struggle for survival, slowly losing their emerald green color and turning

1

a brittle tan, leaving a dead skeleton of their former selves among the barren, broken acres of the coal region.

The once green earth is now shriveled into a jumbled mass of hard, rutted ground—almost colorless. When the scouring, hot wind is just right you can smell the stringent, oily scent of Mine Seven miles before you come to it. The coal dust moves with the raw wind, settling on, and smothering the life out of everything it touches.

Mine seven is only one of twenty coal mines scattered haphazardly in every direction in the Wapakonetka coal field. A spider web of railroad tracks covers the region with spur tracks curving and thrusting towards the unseen mines. Unknowingly, mine seven is about to change hundreds of peoples lives forever. The old ways and the new are moving towards one another and about to collide. They say too much change is as destructive as too little, but there is always the absolute need for change for those who have to survive—but there are those who have an absolute need for things to stay the same so *they* can survive.

The summer days had just begun, and the humid air caused you to sweat even though you were standing still or sitting still. And this July of 1927 was to be one of blood and sacrifice for the beast-of-burden miners, their women, their children, and for the iron-heeled robber barons who ruled over them.

———————

The shrill scream was heard exactly at twenty minutes past five in the morning. The steam whistle at the mine let the miners know their workday would soon begin—6 a.m. to 6 p.m.—be a minute late and you lost an hour's pay. The whistle ceased as abruptly as it had started.

The steep, hilly landscape of mine seven was riddled with tunnels and shafts that plunged hundreds of feet into the sunless earth. The mine buildings were of all shapes and sizes giving the area the look of a tiny city. Long lines of coal cars stood waiting with their precious anthracite coal, and for powerful locomotives to come and rush them to the large, hungry cities and factories that depended on the black cargo to keep them alive and growing. Thousands upon thousands of tons of it made the Harwick Coal Company a giant, and the owner, Brewster Harwick, one of the richest coal barons in America.

Some of the dirty, scarred mine buildings housed hugh steam engines that supplied the power to haul the mine cars up and down the slopes, or lower iron cages crammed with men deep into the black pits. The pump houses, with their massive pumps, pulled water from deep within the shafts to keep them from flooding. Another engine house ran the gigantic roaring fans used to circulate clean air through the ventilation systems of the stagnant, hot tunnels; the ground never ceasing to vibrate. There was the boiler house—the heart that pumped the precious steam through heavy insulated pipes to all the working engines and machinery.

There were rows of other buildings, some two-storey, some three— a blacksmith's shop for repairing and maintaining tools and other equipment; a carpenter's shop, a sawmill for processing lumber for the shafts and tunnels; a powder shed was buried deep in a hillside and held boxes and boxes of dynamite, fuses and blasting caps. Narrow walk-ways, narrow trestles, and conveyor belts criss-crossed the maze of drainage ditches of filthy, oily water.

Dominating it all was the monster coal breaker, looking like some immense medieval cathedral, dark and forbidding as the landscape behind it, its metal roofs running for hundreds of feet downward like a ski jump. When operating, the breaker crushed and separated the coal with a grinding hunger, always surrounded by choking clouds of coal dust and drifting dirt. The breakers huge rollers, screen and jigs endlessly divided and drove the broken coal along the steep iron chutes to the waiting coal cars and their steaming locomotives.

Surrounding the mine, and the houses of the workers and their families, were the mountainous heaps of the culm banks—a refuse of rock and slate, and bits of useless coal. Unending ribbons of dust were always drifting up and down the jagged slopes day and night; the culm bank seemed alive—a moving shadow darkening all the life around it.

At exactly 6 a.m. the shrill scream came again, then echoed into silence above the spiny hilltops where the skeletons of long-dead trees creaked in the stiff winds, their bare, gray arms standing out like warped crosses.

The door of the superintendent's office opened and a husky, dark-haired man in a clean brown shirt and corduroy pants came down the short flight of wooden steps and stood scanning the deserted work yards. His sharp eyes clouded with apprehension, and his stomach knotted. The muscles of his smooth young face tightened.

"What's wrong, Mr. McAlister?" said a soft, troubled voice behind him. "Where is every one?"

McAlister turned to the short, frail man standing in the doorway of the office. The man's pale, round face showed as much worry as McAlister's as he rubbed his hands together. His vest was buttoned tight against his chest and his narrow necktie was knotted tightly at his throat. He wore the green cellophane eyeshade of a clerk-account, and his half-moon eyeglasses were almost on the tip of his blue-veined nose.

McAlister made no reply and walked towards the boiler house fifty yards away. Tiny twisting dust devils preceded him across the open ground to where two men stood beside the wide entrance to the boiler house. They were dressed in grimy, soiled overalls, and wore heavy, scarred work boots; their faces, bare chests and bare arms were shiny with sweat. They lounged against the wall of the building, each calmly smoking a hand-rolled cigarette, and watching McAlister stride quickly to them.

"Dolan," said McAlister, to the tall, barrel-chested man, who threw his cigarette down and nodded, "where the hell is everyone? Keep sounding the whistle."

"Won't do no good," replied Dolan, flicking the sweat from his eyebrows with his thick finger.

McAlister and Dolan studied each other a moment, then McAlister turned to the other man; smaller, but muscular, his hatchet-shaped face red and strained as he puffed on his cigarette.

"Fitzpatrick, sound that whistle," ordered McAlister.

Fitzpatrick took the cigarette from his lips and looked anxiously to Dolan for a sign of what to do.

"Won't do no good, Booth," said Dolan in a calm, firm voice. "Better go see Morgan."

"Why?"

"Go see your brother. He'll explain."

Booth gave each man a last searching glance then moved off.

Fitzpatrick took a drag on his stub of a cigarette. "We still going to be relieved end of our shift?"

"Just like always," said Dolan.

"I'm still not sure of this; if we're doing the right thing. I..."

"Don't matter now," said Dolan, moving towards the entrance to the boiler house. "You're in it up to your sweaty little neck."

———————

The agitated little office clerk was still standing in the doorway of the superintendent's office when Booth returned.

"There's trouble, isn't there?" said the clerk, rubbing his hands together. "I knew it, I could feel it."

"Settle down, Metz," replied Booth. "Get on the phone and call Mr. Chase. Try his home first, then his office. Tell him there's trouble at the mine, that I need to speak with him."

"Then can I go home?"

"No. I need you here. Go on now."

Metz scurried into the office, mumbling to himself. Booth walked to a small Model A Ford pickup and got in. Its engine rattled to life and the gears clattered together as the battered and scratched truck headed downhill, its narrow, worn tires leaving a stream of dust behind.

———————

The housing area of mine seven was typical of all miners' housing everywhere in the coal field. Not much care or thought had gone into the construction of it—no more thought than if it were a string of dog kennels. Each house had four rooms, none over twelve feet by twelve feet. At one time the exteriors had been given a quick coat of bright red paint—the cheapest color that could be had at the time. The color had all but faded to nothing in the sun and rain and snow. The wood shingles of the roofs were a bleached gray, and the ends were starting to curl up. A few houses had shabby, paper-thin curtains over the windows, but most had nothing.

But Harwick Coal Company did provide the luxury of running water—cold only—a bath tub and toilet, and coal stove for cooking and heating. The narrow porch at the front of each house was just as weather-beaten and cheaply junked together as the rest of the place. Twenty dollars a month rent was charged, and everybody joked that it was twenty dollars too much. But nobody laughed when they said it. The shanties were laid out in two long rows, facing each other across a wide main street that was powdered dust in the summer, and ankle-deep mud in the winter. A narrow alley separated each structure, and if your next door neighbor sneezed you could open your window and say 'God bless you,' to them.

The wooden sidewalks fronting the houses were of thick planking of different widths nailed in place, badly worn, and heavily scared and cracked. There were no grassy front yards or flower beds, and the meager vegetable gardens at the rear of the houses struggled for existence. What the chickens and roosters didn't pick to death, the roaming dogs dug up in their hunt for gophers; and if anything did survive these assaults, the ever-present coal dust stunted what remained.

At the east end of the housing area was the two-storey boarding house for the single miners—room and board a dollar a day. At the west end was the community hall and company store, and if you didn't like the store prices you could always drive to town and get it, but buying gasoline made the pay envelope thin. There was no school, no church, no hospital; the Harwick Coal Company didn't provide such things; it was a needless expense.

As Booth McAlister's rattling truck entered the far end of the ugly, makeshift town, he slowed until his vehicle was bearly moving. There were equally battered and fragile looking Chevrolets, Fords, Packards, and Hudsons—mostly trucks, but some automobiles—setting in front or at the backs of the houses. Dogs lounged on the sidewalks or under the front porches. Two curious, long-haired mongrels trotted along beside Booth's truck, sniffing and growling, then moved away; it was getting too hot to snap at the tires.

Smoke was coming from most of the rusty tin chimneys of all the houses and rising lazily. Booth became more agitated as his eyes searched for people, but there were none. He increased the speed of the truck and finally came to a stop halfway along the rows of houses. With his uneasiness growing he stopped and got out. The wooden sidewalk creaked under his weight—the only sound on the entire street until a screen door squeaked open. Booth watched his brother step quietly out of his house and onto the front porch. Morgan McAlister's handsome features resembled that of his brother, along with the shiny thick black hair, but Morgan was much thinner, had more muscle, and his skin was pale white from the sunless years of toiling in the bowels of the mine shafts. He was not wearing his work clothes or work boots, just a thin gray shirt and pants, worn and faded from years of soaking and scrubbing. A pair of old, worn shoes were on his feet.

Morgan came to the edge of the porch, put his hands in his pockets, and gave his brother a warm, friendly smile; an embarrassed smile.

Booth began to hear other screen doors opening, and muffled voices. He glanced to his left, then right, as the miners came out of their houses, some remained on the porches, most came out onto the sidewalk. Like Morgan McAlister, none wore their work garb, and their hands were in their pockets. From the doorways and windows, Booth saw the women and children watching intently. From both ends of the long street the miners began walking towards him, slowly and silently. It only too a few minutes before Booth found himself surrounded. He swallowed, ignoring the sweat beading on his forehead, and turned back to Morgan.

"Was this your idea?" asked Booth.

"It was everybody's," replied Morgan, his voice calm and gentle. "You know this has been coming for a long time now."

"You're crazy to go on strike," said Booth. "With the mines in Kentucky and West Virginia and Tennessee out on strike, the demand for coal will go up." He turned to the other miners. "You men will have more work than you can handle."

"That's what we're afraid of," said a voice from the sea of grim faces, and the men couldn't help laughing.

"Chase won't give you a raise, no matter how hard you howl," said Booth loudly.

"It isn't just wages," said Morgan. "We've been working seven days a week for over a year. We were told it would only be temporary."

"Spending twelve and thirteen hours a day working in the pits of hell ain't my idea of temporary," yelled a miner.

"At least you got money coming in every month, don't you?" Booth yelled back.

"Seven dollars and fifty cents a day just keeps our families from starving," replied a miner. "We need to live!"

The whole crowd voiced their agreement.

"Booth," said Morgan, "we've formed a committee, and we want to speak to Chase about our demands."

"And you want me to tell him?"

"You're the mine superintendent."

"And where's this committee of yours?"

"Right here," said Morgan, motioning to some men at the front of the crowd. "You know Tom Mitchell."

Mitchell stepped forward, a man in his late fifties, broad shouldered, but face puffy, eyes watery, and large strong hands. He stifled a cough and held a hand out to Booth. Booth hesitated then shook it.

"I've known you a lot of years, Booth," began Mitchell. "Since the first day you come here. I like you, we all like you. You've always been fair with us. We don't hold anything against you. All these men want is something better for themselves and their families."

"What if you get fired?" replied Booth. "Where you going to find work if you're put on the black list at all the other mines?"

Mitchell smiled, stifled another cough, and said, "Well, before the black list gets me, I think the black lung will. Sometimes it gets so bad at night I have to run outside to breathe; I feel like I'm being strangled to death."

"We're tired of these slave wages," said a miner, stepping up beside Mitchell. "We deserve more, and you know it."

"You on this committee, Pike?" asked Booth.

"That's right."

Kelly Pike was tough and not afraid of anything—his youth saw to that. He was tall and wiry and hard-muscled, and ready for a fight any time. His gray eyes were filled with defiance, and his square jaw was set tight.

Booth smiled. "Ready to take on the whole world, huh?"

"If I have to."

"Be careful the world doesn't kick you in the teeth."

"You be careful your shiny black coal don't turn red with blood."

A threatening grumble came from the tense crowd, letting Booth know they felt the same as Pike.

"Settle down, Kelly," ordered Morgan. "I told you, none of that talk."

"There's already been blood shed," said Dan Ketchum as he stepped forward. He extended his hand, and Booth took it. "No hard feelings, Booth."

Ketchum was stooped shouldered and weary looking. He had hard muscles on him, but his eyes revealed a worn, anxiety-ridden man, old before his time, and his dark blond hair was stained forever from the coal dust of the mine.

"Dan, here, is the last of the committee," said Morgan.

"You said blood has been shed already," said Booth. "When?"

"You forgot so soon?" said Ketchum with a troubled look. "A year ago yesterday, we lost three killed, and nine crippled in the south shaft explosion."

"And Chase and Harwick said it was miners' carelessness," said Pike loudly. "The liars!"

A chorus of "yeahs" exploded from the crowd.

"We got a right to earn a descent wage; our daily bread," said Ketchum earnestly.

"Our daily bread is dried up and rancid," added Pike, his angry eyes still on Booth. "And it stinks of poverty."

Booth and Pike faced each other, waiting for the other to make a move. Morgan stepped off the porch, placing himself between the two.

"Kelly," said Morgan, "step back, we're not here for a brawl."

Pike nodded submissively, took a step back, and Morgan addressed Booth.

"We're not asking for the moon, Booth. We just need to talk with Chase, let him know our demands."

Booth shook his head dejectedly. "You think you can make demands on Chase?"

"Yes," said Morgan strongly. "And on Harwick. We know he arrived here three days ago, that's why we waited till now to walk out. After you tell Chase what's going on, we're willing to go to his office and talk. If Harwick is there, so much the better."

Booth shook his head again in disgust. "And what if you're all fired? Where you going to go, what are you going to do? The company owns these houses, not you people. They own everything but the clothes on your backs. How will you feed your families?"

"We're not backing down," said Morgan. "It's win or die."

"You remember three years ago, the strike in Skullykill, Pennsylvania?" asked Booth quietly. "That was one of Harwick's mines too. You remember what they did there? How many died when the strikebreakers were brought in?"

"We'll wait till the end of the week," said Morgan, unmoved. "Then the strike will be on for as long as it takes."

Booth saw the determination in Morgan, and the others, got in his truck and started the engine. Morgan came up and leaned in the window.

"I'm sorry you had to get in the middle of this, Booth. I really am."

"God help you people," said Booth, and began backing the truck away.

The crowd parted, Booth turned the truck around and drove back towards the mine.

———

As soon as Booth's truck came up the wide, dusty road and squealed to a stop in front of the mine office, Metz hurried out and down the steps. He was more nervous and fidgety than when Booth had left him. He barely gave Booth time to get out of the truck.

"Mr. McAlister, I can't get through. I've been trying and trying."

Metz's whining only irritated Booth more than he was. "What the hell's wrong?" he said angrily.

"The telephone line, it just buzzes and buzzes."

Booth started quickly to the boiler house where Fitzpatrick was pushing a heavy wheel barrow load of coal towards the entrance.

"Fitzpatrick," shouted Booth.

Fitzpatrick set the wheelbarrow down and advanced to meet Booth.

"Any of you people fool with the telephone line?"

"Why should we?" replied Fitzpatrick sourly.

"You destroy company property, you'll go to jail."

"We ain't done nothing to the damn phone line," said Fitzpatrick hotly.

"See that you don't." Booth hurried away.

Metz stood watching as Booth came towards him.

"Don't worry about it, Metz. We've had trouble with the line before."

Booth got in his truck and started it as Metz rushed up.

"Mr. McAlister, what's happening? Where is everyone?"

"Go to the company store, see if that phone is working. If it is stay there, I may need to call you."

"But I don't..."

The truck skidded away leaving Metz shrouded in a wall of rising dust.

———————

Booth's mind was spinning as fast as the narrow tires of his truck as he left mine seven far behind him. He was the mine superintendent, he was supposed to know what was going on, what the miners were thinking, saying, plotting. He wiped the sweat from his eyes as the sun beat down on the black metal roof inches above his head. A stream of dust trailed away behind him like a huge rooster's tail as he increased his speed down the rough gravel road.

After five miles he turned off the main road and drove along a one-lane driveway, packed hard and smooth. It wound through a section of tall, leafy maples, and beyond this Booth could see the steep roof lines of the stately two-storey house in the distance. He slowed the truck as he entered the spacious grounds surrounding Addison Chase's mansion. The deep green lawns, perfectly manicured , looked unreal, as did the large sparkling pond with two snow-white swans gliding gracefully from one side to the other.

The elaborately built house was of thick blocks of light gray stone, streaked here and there with the foliage of brilliant green ivy clinging to the walls. The brick chimneys of four fireplaces stood out sharply against the bright blue sky. But the corner towers, and the Gothic architecture, made the house appear more like a somber monastery. Narrow, eight-foot-high windows, with pointed peaks seemed to want to shut out the light, not let it in. Even now, with the sunlight touching parts of it, dark shadows made the house seem deserted and lifeless.

Booth drove slowly along the circular drive to the front of the house and stopped, and the truck's engine chattered into silence after a few seconds. Booth moved quickly up the long flight of wide stone steps to the hand carved double doors. He tapped the large brass knocker loudly and ran his shirt sleeve over his damp face and hair. It wasn't long before a thin, meek woman in a maid's uniform opened the door.

"May I help you?"

"Is Mr. Chase here, please?"

"I'm not sure, I'll…"

"Who is it, Elinor?" asked a female voice.

The maid bowed her head and stepped back as Isabel Chase approached.

"It's me, Mrs. Chase. Booth McAlister from mine seven." He gave a quick smile and bow of his head as the maid had done.

Isabel ran her small, cold blue eyes over Booth from head to foot. She was a tall, slender woman with silky silver hair, and an attractive face, pale and smooth and lifeless as marble. But she had the aurora of a queen.

"I need to see Mr. Chase," continued Booth. "It's very important. The phone at the mine isn't…"

"Yes, the phone here isn't working either. Just noise. My son left early for the office. I'm sure he's in Palmyra by now."

"Then I'll see him there," said Booth, backing away. "Sorry to have bothered you."

"Is there anything wrong?" asked Isabel, studying Booth's bright red face.

"No, ma'am. Just mine business. Thank you."

Booth turned and hurried to his truck. Isabel closed the door, but stood staring through the thick beveled glass. Her sharp eyes held on Booth as the speed of his truck increased rapidly down the driveway.

"Elinor," called Isabel without turning from the door.

"Yes, ma'am?" answered the maid, coming across the large entrance hall towards her.

"Is the telephone working yet?"

"I'll have to check, Mrs. Chase."

"See if you can reach my son at his office."

"Right away, Mrs. Chase."

———————

The town of Palmyra was fifteen miles further along the curving, dusty main road. Booth forced the accelerator pedal of his truck almost to the floor, but eased up every once in a while when the engine clattered a little too loud. A whiff of steam began to appear from under the radiator cap. The back of Booth's shirt was stained with sweat from the humid air, and sweat trickled from his armpits down his ribs. He kept glancing at the temperature gauge on the dash board, and at the fluttering steam escaping from the radiator.

"Keep going, sweetheart," he muttered softly. "Keep going." His throat was dry and his hands wet on the warm steering wheel.

It was still early when he reached Palmyra. The town hadn't really come alive yet. There were a few farmers' trucks piled high with produce they were bringing in to sell, and other trucks with crated produce on their way to the train depot to be loaded. The bright colored brick stores and homes and office buildings lined the wide, paved streets, north, south, east and west. It was a thriving town thanks to the farms and the coal field.

Harwick Coal Company had created the town, kept it growing and prosperous. There was a new hospital, a library, two churches, and a three-storey courthouse with a white-faced clock at the top of its center tower; a clock you could see an entire block away. But no one gave much thought to the dangerous, dirty mines, and the army of slaving miners that really gave Palmyra its life's blood.

Booth drove his truck to the front of a two-storey brick office building—the home of Harwick Coal. The rickety pickup shuttered as the engine went dead. The radiator was hissing stream straight into the air as Booth crossed the concrete sidewalk and entered the building.

The coolness of the building's lobby soothed Booth's tension somewhat, and he proceeded up the shiny, multi-colored marble stairs to the second floor. The fancy wrought iron railing was even cool and soothed his hot hand. The ceiling fans were swirling silently about him, their breezes brushing his flushed face.

When Booth opened the door to the large outer office of Addison Chase's office, he was met with a flurry of activity. Telephones were ringing and clerks were skirring back and forth among the desks, talking quickly and efficiently to one another; others were searching through tall wooden filing cabinets; other clerks typed rapidly creating neat, umblemished reports. A long, polished walnut railing separated this work area from the waiting area. On the far side of this small mob of workers was President Chase's office, encased all around in gritty, frosted glass panels, giving the large room absolute privacy.

A slender, bald-headed clerk rushed forward, intercepting Booth before he could cross the waiting area.

"Yes, what is it?" asked the clerk, his narrow suspicious eyes taking close note of Booth's dusty, worn clothing and scuffed boots.

"I need to see Mr. Chase."

"Is he expecting you?"

"I'm the superintendent of mine seven. I have to speak with Mr. Chase, it can't wait."

"I'm afraid it will have to," said the clerk dryly. "Mr. Chase is busy. If you give me your name, and have a seat, I'll…"

"No, I won't have a seat," shouted Booth.

The entire office dropped into silence, except for the ringing of a telephone, and the loud ticking of a pendulum clock on the far wall. The slender clerk, and the other clerks, remained still, not sure if they should move or not. They stared at Booth as if he were some vicious dog that had wandered in.

"I don't have time to wait," said Booth, calming himself. "Tell Mr. Chase there is trouble at mine seven. Unless you want to take the responsibility for what happens."

The slender clerk tilted his small, bald head back, displaying a defiant pinched chin. "Well," he said coldly, "if its important mine business, I'm sure Mr. Chase will want to know about it."

"I'm sure he will," replied Booth, his angry gaze still boring into the clerk's eyes.

With obvious contempt, the little man turned and walked to the door of Chase's office. He knocked softly, then opened it after a voice said, "yes". He stuck his head just inside and spoke softly.

Booth threw a glance at the other clerks, still watching him, and they went quickly back to work. The slender, bald-headed clerk then motioned to Booth to come to him.

Addison Chase's office was large and very Spartan. There was a wide mahogany desk and padded leather chair in the center of the room. A shiny black telephone set near the left corner of the polished desk. Two plain wooden chairs were against one wall, and a long leather sofa against the opposite wall; a coat rack and umbrella stand next to it. No scenic pictures or photographs of any kind hung on the walls; no sun shades on the windows. The dull, light green walls gave the room a sense of coolness and drabness.

Seated at the gleaming desk, Addison Chase concentrated on a business letter he was composing, his fountain pen scratching across the smooth white paper. The only other sound in the room was the low hum of the ceiling fan. The three large windows behind him were shut, and despite the growing warmth, Chase was dressed neatly and richly in a four-button, blue pin-striped suit, white shirt and blue silk tie. He looked much younger than his thirty years, boyish almost; his wavy brown hair had a sheen to it, but his thin face was pale, sickly looking, and his long fingers looked delicate. His neatly trimmed moustache gave him a dashing appearance, like a Hollywood movie star, but his light blue eyes—his mother's eyes—were cold and humorless. His gentle manner of speaking was only a façade hiding the hard, unyielding inner presence of a gladiator of business.

As Addison concentrated on his letter the slender clerk opened the door wider and admitted Booth.

"Mr. Chase," said the clerk, "this is Superintendent McAlister," then stepped back, closing the door quietly.

Addison finished scribbling a last sentence, set his fountain pen down and looked up. Booth couldn't help noticing the same dominating gaze he had seen in the eyes of Isabell Chase—that predator gaze. Addison gave a faint smile and leaned back in his chair.

"My clerk, Mr. Jeffers, said you were very agitated and needed to see me about some mine business."

Booth remained at the office door, unsure whether to come forward. "Yes, Mr. Chase," he began. "I would have telephoned, but the line at the office is…"

"Yes, I tried phoning my house a few minutes ago, same thing. What is it you wanted?"

Booth came forward, giving a helpless shrug, and stopped at the front of the desk. "The miners have walked out."

"They're calling a strike?" said Addison, his expression turning grim.

"Not exactly, no."

"Then what are they doing?"

Though Addison's voice was soft, Booth could feel the words pressing against him like a sharp stick to his stomach.

"The committee said they'll wait till the end of the week to...to see if you or Mr. Harwick will sit down with them and...hear their demands. If not, they'll strike; shut down the mine."

"How did this happen, McAlister?"

"Sir?" said Booth, puzzled.

"Did this situation just spring up out of the ground, overnight?"

"I'm not sure, sir."

"You're the superintendent. Don't you hear things, don't you talk to people? Why didn't you know about this beforehand?"

"It was a complete surprise, Mr. Chase. I would have done something if..."

"Who's the head of this committee you mentioned?"

"My brother, Morgan."

Addison shook his head slowly. "Obviously you don't talk to your brother either."

"What do you need me to do, Mr. Chase?"

"First, I want you to make a list of the names of this so-called committee."

"There's only four, sir."

"Good." A frown suddenly came to Addison's face. "Are there any union agitators involved in this?"

"No."

"You sure?"

"It's just the miners, sir."

"If there are union agitators behind this, you know what's going to happen out there, don't you?"

"I warned them, Mr. Chase."

"All our coal fields are non-union, and that's the way they'll stay."

"I agree, Mr. Chase. But if you'd just talk with my brother, I'm sure…"

"I'm not talking to your brother, or any committee. And neither will Mr. Harwick. He's just come down from Chicago for the summer, to relax, not negotiate with a bunch of whining strikers."

"What do you want me to do, Mr. Chase?"

"Absolutely nothing. Go back and make sure the mine is secure. If you need help, I'll see you get it. Sheriff Deets and his deputies can handle the situation."

"I'm not so sure, Mr. Chase."

"Why not?"

"I talked to these men this morning. They're not going to knuckle under, like they used to. There's something more going on. It's not just pay and shorter hours they…"

"I don't care what it is, or what you think it is. Go back, secure the mine, and keep me informed. I'll let you know what's to be done." Addison picked up his pen and began writing.

Booth waited, then started to go, but turned back. "If I'd have known what my brother and the others were up to I…"

"It doesn't matter now, does it?" said Addison, without looking up.

"Even though he's my brother, the mine comes first, I know. I'm the superintendent, and…"

"Then do your job," replied Addison, still writing his letter.

"I always do, Mr. Chase. Thank you for seeing me."

Addison made no reply, picked up his letter and began studying it. Booth stared at him, uneasy and cowed before this man of power, the man who had control over his life, and the lives of hundreds and hundreds of miners in the Harwick coal fields. But at the same moment Booth couldn't help hating him for treating him with such contempt; like he wasn't worth talking to—wasn't worth anything.

After Booth had gone, Addison set the letter down and stared into space, his expression troubled. He pressed a small button to the right of the desk. Seconds later, Jeffers, the head clerk, rushed in.

"Yes, Mr. Chase?"

"Have my car brought around, I'm going to Mr. Harwick's."

"Right away, Mr. Chase."

———————

The roomy, five-passenger Buick touring car hummed gently along the graveled country road, its low, graceful body lines shedding the thin streaming dust out and away before it could reach the open windows. Addison sat in the plush rear seat, fanning himself lazily with his gray bowler hat as the uniformed chauffeur concentrated on the road ahead.

When the car came to the turn-off leading to Addison's house, it turned in the opposite direction and proceeded along another more carefully kept gravel road—a private road that wound through acres of Sycamore trees, then bushy, long-limbed pines. The road rose gently and steadily until it came over a rise, then there it was—Harwick Hall—looking more like a castle than a summer home; occupied only four months out of the year.

The intricate wooden scrollwork framing row upon row of tall front windows reflected the blinding glare of the morning sun out across the well kept lawns and flower gardens. Round, three-storey towers, and square three-storey towers dominated the sides and rear of the Hall. Lofty pine trees were spaced exactly twenty feet apart along the arrow-straight driveway which swept gracefully to beneath the front portico. There were two marble pillars on each side of the portico, and perched atop each pillar were crouching, dragon-faced gargoyles to scare away the Devil and his evil; but most of the miners in the Harwick Coal fields said it was to warn you of the devil within.

Addison only had to wait a few moments after ringing the entrance bell before one of the ten-foot-high hand carved doors was opened, its little rosettes of bright stained glass glinting in the sunlight like blood-red wine.

"Mr. Chase," said the white-coated manservant, giving a quick bow, "how nice to see you again."

"And you," said Addison, handing the man his hat, and entering the immense entrance hall. "Is he up yet?"

"Having breakfast now, sir."

"I need to see him. It's urgent."

"Right this way, please."

Brewster Harwick, dressed in a loose fitting red silk robe, trimmed with black piping and black sash, sat gnawing on a thick pork chop, his fingers greasy from the thick golden fat. The sixteen-foot long dining table was covered with a snow-white linen table cloth, embroidered with a fancy leaf design. High-backed Gothic style chairs surrounded the table. A tall bouquet of pink and white roses stood up from the center of an enormous round silver bowl like a mound of hay. Ornate mirrors and gold stitched oriental draperies lined the two long side walls, making the room seem twice as large as it was. In each corner of the room a sculpted African slave—life size—held a glimmering gold candelabrum high above his bowed head.

Brewster's bulky six-foot frame filled the high-backed chair he was in. His large round head was covered with a thin, neatly combed layer of black hair, and his puffy red lips gave him the appearance of a decadent Roman emperor. He was only fifty, but looked older—looked wary—looked cruel. He belched loudly, dropped the pork chop bone onto his plate and dug into a bowl of biscuits and dark gravy with a gold spoon.

Addison sat quietly at the far end of the table, hands folded on his lap, patiently watching Brewster feed. Finally: "So do you agree on what I want to do, Brewster?"

"Let me think, let me think," said Brewster, jabbing his spoon in Addison's direction. "If those sons-a-bitches have joined up with one of those goddamn Red, agitator unions…"

"I don't think it's come to that."

"There's no need for unions," said Brewster angrily. "They get a foothold in any business they'll destroy the goddamn country!"

"I agree."

"Then handle this thing quick. If you have to replace every one of those bastards out there, do it. I own that mine, that coal, and those houses they wallow in. I own them! If you have to bring up a trainload of niggers from the South, do it. They'll work for a dollar a day, and kiss your ass to get."

"I don't think we have to do anything like that. Not yet anyway."

"Clara!" hollered Brewster. "Clara!"

A uniformed maid hurried through a door at the far end of the room, her starched white apron rustling against her deep green dress. Before she could reach the table Brewster's hard voice stopped her.

"Another pork chop."

"Yes, Mr. Brewster."

"And a couple of big sausages," he yelled.

"Right away, Mr. Brewster," she said, and disappeared into the kitchen.

"Did I tell you I own a bank now," said Brewster, dumping two spoonfuls of sugar into his coffee cup.

"No," said Addison with a faint smile. "You'll own half of Chicago the rate you're going."

"That's no a bad idea," said Brewster, grinning. He took a gulp of his coffee, picked up his spoon and attacked the biscuits and gravy again.

Addison closed his eyes a moment, seeking relief from the gluttonous scene, then forced a smile, saying, "How are Abigail and the children?"

Brewster gave a quick grunt. "She's already harping about being here. The weather's too hot, nothing to do, nowhere to go. Nothing's ever right for her."

"Yes, she always was a city girl."

"Well, now she can be a country girl."

"The children are what, eight or nine now?"

"I guess." Brewster pointed his spoon at Addison. "For God's sake, stay single. And never have children. If you do, drown them right away."

Addison rose from his chair. "I'd better be getting back. I say we let the miners sit. Once their money and food begin to run out, we won't have to negotiate anything."

"Just get them in a corner, then kick hell out of them."

"They're already in a corner, only they don't know it."

"Get them back to work or get rid of them."

"If things get out of hand we can always call in the National Guard."

"Hell no! That means bringing in Hallgren. That son-of-a-bitch shouldn't be governor of anything. He should be in prison with the rest of those thieves at the state capitol."

Addison couldn't help laughing. "True, but he's been helpful to us in the past."

"His old man was as foul and corrupt as he is," continued Brewster. "Made all his money after World War One, running illegal whiskey up from Mexico to every gin mill in the U.S. Have to hand it to the rotten bastard though, he made millions. Booze and whore houses."

"Hallgren can still be a powerful ally if we need him," replied Addison.

"Let me ask you something," said Brewster, grabbing a butter knife, slicing off a thick chunk of butter from its dish, and mashing it into a pile of crispy hash browns on his plate. "How big are our coal fields here in Ohio?"

"Little over two hundred square miles," said Addison.

"How much do they make a year?"

"Between forty and forty-five million."

"You know what Andrew Carnegie sold his steel corporation for, before the little bastard died?"

"Close to…"

"Exactly two hundred and fifty million. If I had that much money I could be governor myself. I could become richer than Carnegie. Why shouldn't I? There's no such thing as too much money. Anybody ever tells you that, you're talking to an idiot."

"With money like that you could own, not only Chicago, but America," said Addison with a patronizing grin.

"Why not?" said Brewster seriously. "Why shouldn't a select few own it all? When you have the money, the power, and a handful of greedy, gutter-rat senators and congressmen in Washington in your hip pocket, anything's possible."

"Well", said Addison, putting on his hat, "you take care of America, and I'll take care of mine seven."

Brewster wiped his greasy mouth and hands on a large linen napkin and stood up. "Harwick Coal is in the business of making money," he said, "not pampering ignorant, uneducated work mules. Work mules are expendable."

"I agree," replied Addison, "but I don't want a strike that'll get out of hand. I'd rather use a rapier than a sledge hammer."

"I don't want this spreading to the other mines."

"I'm sending Deets and his deputies out there; apply a little pressure, see what happens."

"Crush the bastards," said Brewster moving towards a curved staircase leading to the second floor. "I've got to change and get over to Malabar Farm before it gets too hot."

"Picking tomatoes, are we?" asked Addison.

Brewster laughed and turned back. "Pheasant hunting."

"I didn't know the season was on?"

"It is now," answered Brewster with a grin. "Damn, you should have seen the six-point buck out in the field last night. He shows up again I'll have him in my meat locker. You like deer meat?"

"Not really."

"God, how I love the heart and liver. Ever skin out a deer?"

"Haven't had the pleasure, I'm afraid."

"Fascinating. That thin, razor-sharp blade slicing away. The belly opens up and the guts flop out on the ground like a big balloon full of water and blood. And the scent of the blood. Love it." Brewster could see Addison wasn't enjoying the skinning details, and looking a bit pale. He slapped his hands together, with a laugh, and started up the stairs. "I'll bring you some pheasant," he called over his shoulder. "You'll enjoy boiling and plucking them." He laughed louder this time.

"Yes," said Addison to himself, "I can hardly wait."

"Call Deets," yelled Brewster from the top of the stairs. "Get him out there!"

Addison watched Brewster's broad, silk covered form move along the upstairs landing. He felt resentful and insulted at being treated like one of the servants—he always had.

CHAPTER 2

The next morning the sun was just breaking over the dark, spiny hills high up behind mine seven. Already the heat was unusually oppressive. The Ford Phaeton touring car came speeding along the road leading into the west end of the housing area. The car's top was folded down, and the oilcloth seats and thick glass windshield were growing hot as the sun beat down.

Sheriff Curtis Deets was driving, his face grim with determination and apprehension. He wore a stiff Stetson hat of a rusty brown color, and a suit and tie to match. He had a holster and revolver buckled to his waist. A sober-faced deputy sat to his right with two large bundles of letter-sized paper on the floorboard between his feet. He pulled his slouch hat lower on his forehead to keep the wind from snatching it. Two other deputies, in the rear seat, clutched large-bore shotguns between their knees, the ominous barrels pointed skyward. No conversation passed between the four; their eyes were on the distant houses, wondering if there were many miners out on the street yet, and if they were armed.

Deets turned the steering wheel sharply as he passed the community hall and sped down the wide main street separating the two long rows of houses. His alert eyes glanced from house to house, and he wiped the sweat from his thick salt and pepper moustache. From the look on his face he was a man given a mission he didn't want to perform. The deputies in the rear seat flicked the safety catches of their shotguns to the "off" position.

Deets slowed the car, several dogs began barking from the front porches, others ran out into the street sniffing at the passing vehicle, eyeing these different smelling strangers. The deputy to Deets's right began tossing handfuls of the letter-sized papers out onto the sidewalk. Some of the miners, and their wives, sitting on their porches, came out to the wooden walk, along with scattered groups of barefoot children. The children laughed and grabbed at the fluttering sheets of paper as if it were some sort of game. Before Deets had reached the end of the long, dusty street and turned around to come back, more men, women, and children appeared at the screen doors and windows of the houses, then began to come outside.

Deets increased his speed a little. The deputy continued throwing out the sheets of paper. The deputies in the rear gripped their shotguns more tightly. Before Deets could get halfway back along the street, a large crowd had formed, blocking his path. He brought the car to a stop. He and his deputies waited anxiously. The men, women, and children just stared quietly. More people began to assemble behind the car, then Deets began to hear angry mumbling.

"Sheriff?" said a strong voice.

Deets looked quickly to his right and saw Morgan McAlister walking towards him with one of the sheets of paper in his hand.

"What do you think you're doing?" asked Morgan.

Deets forced a defiant grin. "You can read, can't you? It's an eviction notice. You're trespassing on private property. You don't want to work here you don't have to live here."

"Go to hell, Deets," yelled a miner, and a chorus of loud voices agreed with him.

"And you can go to jail you start anything," Deets hollered back.

A defiant grumble came from the crowd. Deets and the deputies could see more people coming their way from both ends of the street now.

"Does Chase think he can bluff us with this?" asked Morgan calmly, holding up the eviction notice.

"Mr. Chase and Mr. Harwick don't have time for you people," replied Deets.

"No? Then what are you and your men doing here?"

"Giving you your first…and last warning. Go back to work or start packing your suitcase."

"And if we don't?"

"You know what'll happen," answered Deets, ominously.

Tom Mitchell came out of the crowd and walked up beside Morgan. "Curtis," he said gently, "why you doing this? We're only trying to survive; turn our lives into something better."

"The go back to work," said Deets angrily. "Or you're all going to starve to death."

"You don't look very good, Curtis," said Mitchell. "You shouldn't take your job so serious."

"Well, you don't look any better than I do, Tom."

"That's what a mining life will do to you. We haven't been fishing together for a long time, we…"

"There ain't going to be any time for fishing. I know you're a member of this so-called committee. I don't hold it against you, but I've been given orders about you people."

"Why do you say it that way?" asked Dan Ketchum as he came up behind Mitchell.

"Say what?"

"You people," replied Ketchum. "Like…like we're different from you, and Chase, and Harwick. Why, because we're poor and dig in the earth to keep from starving? Because we don't wear fancy hats and suits?"

"Look, Dan," said Deets, taking off his hat and wiping the sweat pouring down his forehead, "I don't like this situation any better than you. But you people got to realize you got no say in this, even if you think you do. You're going out of here."

"We ain't going out of here, you are," said an angry voice, and the huge crowd agreed.

It was Kelly Pike who had spoken. He shoved his way between Mitchell and Ketchum, and stood almost nose to nose with Deets.

"Mr. Pike," said Deets in a friendly, mocking tone. "Haven't seen you in my drunk tank for quite a while. Don't get to town much any more, do you?"

"Next time I come to town, it'll be to shove your fat head through a window of your own jail."

Pike took a step forward and the two deputies with the shotguns stood up, their fingers on the triggers of their guns.

"Kelly, that's enough," said Morgan, putting a hand on Pike's arm, causing him to step back.

The only sound now was the throbbing engine of Deets's car. Finally he glanced over his shoulder to the deputies. "Sit down."

Morgan stepped up to the car and leaned on the door, and spoke gently. "These men have worked this mine most of their lives; brought out trainload after trainload of coal with their sweat and muscle. Some even died getting it out. Chase and Harwick have no idea what our world here is like. Every man feels this mine belongs to him, and we're not going to leave go of it just because you come in here throwing a few pieces of paper around."

Deets stared at Morgan, almost with sympathy, glanced at the people around him, then back to Morgan. "Just because you're the mine boss here, don't mean you can control this situation. You're wasting your time, and you're wasting my gasoline making me sit here."

"Then I guess you better go," said Morgan, stepping back.

"We'll be back."

"We'll be here."

Deets gunned the engine of the car, but the densely packed crowd never moved. Deets looked to Morgan.

Morgan raised his hand. "Let 'em pass."

The crowd slowly parted and Deets's car proceeded up the street.

"Put us off if you can," shouted Pike.

The men and women crumpled the eviction notices tightly in their hands, and began tossing them in front of Deets's car as it passed. The children joined in, grinning from ear to ear.

The crowd began to disperse as Morgan returned to the porch of his house and sat on the top step. The screen door squeaked open and a lovely, slender woman came out. Katherine McAlister's golden brown hair was cut short and her dark brown eyes held a touch of sadness in them as she watched Morgan. Her thin, faded cotton dress clung to her firm, youthful body. She sat down beside Morgan and wrapped an arm around his.

"Well, husband," she said, "that was short and to the point." Her low, sultry voice held a touch of humor, and Morgan smiled.

"At least we got a rise out of old Chase. That's good."

"Think he'll talk to you?"

"It's either that or the mine stays closed."

Morgan glanced at the eviction notice he still held, crumpled it up and tossed it away.

Tom Mitchell, Dan Ketchum and Kelly Pike walked up and threw their notices down also.

"Looks like we're in for it," said Mitchell, rubbing the stubby, tough whiskers on his pudgy face. "But we figured on that."

Morgan smiled. "If Chase and Harwick weren't worried, they wouldn't have sent Deets. We made a move, they made a move."

"But this isn't a game of checkers," said Ketchum, worry in his voice. "This eviction thing is…"

"Don't worry about something that ain't happened," replied Morgan.

"Fine," said Pike, "but if Deets and his goons want to start waving guns around, we should do the same."

"No," said Morgan forcefully. "That's the last thing we need to do."

"Morgan's right, Kelly," said Katherine. "There can't be no war here. Think of the children. You young bucks are always ready to fight at the drop of a hat."

Mitchell laughed, saying, "That's why he's always getting tossed in jail."

The others grinned, but Pike's face remained stern as he replied, "We got to keep this strike moving. We can't back down or we're done for."

"He's right there," said Mitchell. "We can't strike for long, so we'll have to strike hard."

"Remember four years ago?" said Ketchum. "That mine in Pennsylvania? They went out for seven months, and when it was over they were worse off than before."

"We can't stay out for that long," said Morgan.

"We should have hoarded up more food, before doing this," said Ketchum anxiously. "Waited another three or four months maybe."

"That wouldn't do any good," said Morgan. "Then we'd be into winter. We can't survive a winter strike."

"And all the miners' savings are already at the bottom of the barrel," said Mitchell.

"What about getting one of those miners' unions involved in this?" asked Ketchum.

"Ah, hell," snapped Pike, "they're useless. Soon as a union shows up in the coal fields they give loud-mouth speeches then the coal owners beat, starve, and drive the miners out, and you never hear from the union again. All they're after is your dues money so they can go on giving fancy promises, and filling their gut with big meals and whiskey."

"But I heard these unions got a strike fund," said Ketchum. "A dollar a day they give the strikers."

"Christ Almighty, Dan," said Mitchell, "we're scratching to say alive now. What the hell we going to do on a dollar a day?"

"Besides," said Morgan, "we've never begged or expected charity from outside. We always worked hard for what we got, and were proud of it. We don't need outside help."

"Okay," said Ketchum, not really convinced, "but what about contacting the other mines in the coal field? See if they'll go out too."

"I thought about it," said Morgan, "but they're worse off than we are, and we can't waste time trying to convince them to come in with us. We have to do this on our own. Come hell or high water."

"Amen," said Pike. "We don't have to beg nobody for help. Why not make Chase and Harwick beg? What about all those miners that have come through here year after year? They get maimed or crippled up, and they're sent on their way became Chase and Harwick can't get any more work out of them; they're tossed out like so much garbage."

"Kelly's right," said Katherine. "We can't just stand aside and let that happen to any more of our people; to be sent off without nothing but the clothes on their backs. We've got to hold together, like one great family, or we won't survive this."

"What if we start running out of money?" said Ketchum. "Out of food?"

"You could stand to lose a little weight," said Mitchell, jabbing Ketchum in the belly with his thumb.

Ketchum knocked the hand away. "This ain't nothing to joke about, Tom."

"Dan," said Morgan, "don't worry about the hunger in your stomach, that's not anything. Worry about getting something better for yourself and your family. When you get old and too lame to work, who's going to take care of your wife and kids?"

"It sure as hell won't be Chase," said Pike. "If we have to suffer and die for this, let's do it."

"We'll wait the five days for Chase or Harwick to talk with us," said Morgan. "Then we'll close off the mine until they do talk."

"We'll have to," said Mitchell.

"It's our mine, not theirs," said Pike.

Ketchum simply shrugged, still filled with apprehension.

After Mitchell, Pike, and Ketchum had gone on home, Morgan and Katherine remained seated on the porch steps in silence. She could sense Morgan was deeply troubled; the walk-out had been his idea, and now all the miners and their families were relying on his judgment to win out against whatever odds that came.

"What about some breakfast?" said Katherine. "You haven't had any yet."

Morgan shook his head. "Not hungry."

"Then let's take a walk before it gets much hotter." She ran her fingers through his shiny black hair.

"Sounds good."

As they moved leisurely along the wooden sidewalk, Morgan's eyes surveyed the activity of the neighborhood. There were children playing tag to the accompaniment of a frisking, barking dog, women were washing clothes in large wooden wash tubs, others tending their meager vegetable gardens at the rear of the tattered houses. Men were lounging in the shade of porch roofs or leaning against porch railings talking and laughing—acting as if everything were normal—nothing to worry about.

"I've got a lot of faith in you, Morgan," Katherine said finally. "So does everyone else. Women and children included."

"I know, that's why I've got this great hard lump in my belly. And it won't go away. And it scares me. I can't let these people down. It was different when we were only planning this. Just talk. Now it's time to do battle."

"And be courageous," said Katherine. "The miners especially. The women and children look to you men to be brave. The men can't break; they've got to stay strong, fight for their families, give them hope, keep them safe. All of this has to be more than just about wages, and less hours in the pits. We need a better future to look forward to. We need our own homes, not company homes. A lot of these miners can't even read or write; their wives either. All any of us have ever known is unending struggle."

"And the children go barefoot and in threadbare clothing," said Morgan. "They shouldn't have to."

Two seven-year-old girls, with streaming yellow hair and sun tanned faces, came running along the dusty street, trying to keep a fragile homemade kite in the air. Their thin, patched dresses clung to them in the hot breeze.

"Look at what we made, Katherine," yelled one of the girls.

"It's wonderful," Katherine called out, her face bright and smiling. She stopped and watched the children race on up the street, laughing.

Morgan put his arm around her and they walked on. A look of sadness came into Katherine's face.

"The only time I see you smile like that," said Morgan, "is when you're around these children."

"I guess that's because I miss ours so much."

"So do I," said Morgan softly.

"I'm sorry, Morgan."

"No. Don't say that."

"When you lose two beautiful angels like we had," said Katherine, "it does something to you."

"I know."

"To see them die from polio, a year a part, and there was nothing we could do." Katherine shook her head to hold back her tears. "I couldn't go through that again, ever. I'd rather die myself."

"It broke my heart too," said Morgan, pressing her tightly to him. "But we're all right now. We're doing better."

They walked on, each lost in their own thoughts, clinging to each other, their throats tight with emotion.

"Let's go back," said Morgan. "It's getting hot."

Turning to start back, Katherine looked across the street to Booth McAlister's house. It was larger than all the others, and better kept up as it was the superintendent's residence; and he made much more money than a simple coal miner.

There was the dark silhouette of someone at one of the large windows, then a lace curtain was pulled in place and the figure was gone.

"That looked like Hope," said Katherine.

"This strike's going to be hard on her and Booth," said Morgan, looking at the house. "Everyone's already shying away from them because he has to report to Chase. But he'll manage."

"What about Hope?" asked Katherine. "I hardly ever see her out any more. Have you talked with her?"

"I tried a couple of times, at the company store. But it's useless. You know how she feels. She's never going to change."

"You should try any way. She's still your sister."

Morgan forced a smile. "If you insist. Come on, let's have that breakfast you talked about."

They walked on up the street at a brisk walk, and the lace curtain over the window parted. Hope McAlister stood looking out again, watching Morgan and Katherine. Her large amber eyes held an intense, unmistakable bitterness. She was dressed neatly in a plain white blouse, and her long black skirt reached almost to her ankles. Her bright chestnut brown hair was coiled tightly in a bun at the back of her head. Her face was smooth like satin, and exquisite, except for the deep, razor-thin lines at the corners of her mouth and eyes, caused by years of gnawing anger. When she started away from the window, the shoes on her slender feet shuffled across the carpet, and she balanced herself by a cane in each hand.

The interior of the large house was dark and cool and silent, except for the drone of a large metal fan perched on the fireplace mantel. The furniture was highly polished, the sofa and chairs thickly padded with a rich floral pattern of dark colors. The framed pictures on the walls—each one depicting a bouquet of flowers was also of dark, somber colors and in an imitation of an oil painting.

Hope shuffled to the doorway of the kitchen and stood looking at Booth. He was seated at the small square table, a glass of whiskey in his hand, and the bottle before him. He stared into space a moment then took a sip from the glass.

"Having breakfast, are you?" said Hope.

Booth just glanced at her and took another sip.

"I just saw Morgan and Katherine go by," said Hope.

"So?"

"You just going to sit there and drink, and let him take this mine away from you?"

"It's not my mine. It belongs to Harwick."

"You're the superintendent. Chase expects you to do something."

"What?" answered Booth, pouring himself another drink. "These miners aren't going to listen to me now."

"That's because Morgan has turned them against you. Your own brother did this, behind your back."

"These men are tired of working like abused plow mules. I can't hold that against them."

"You should have known about this before it happened. You could have gone to Chase and stopped it."

"Well, I didn't know," said Booth, and slammed his glass on the table.

Hope crossed to the table and stood staring at Booth. He refused to look up, waiting for her to go away.

"What are you going to do if you lose your job here?" said Hope bitterly. "He has no right to do this."

"No matter what he does, he's still our brother, and…"

"He's your brother, not mine," said Hope viciously.

Booth lunged to his feet, knocking his chair over, and started out of the kitchen.

"He'll destroy you," said Hope loudly.

Booth turned back. "This is none of your concern. Whatever happens will happen whether you like it or not. You have no control over it any more than I do."

"I've spent ten years here, cooking and cleaning, and taking care of things. You could at least show some backbone. You going to let your brother and these miners ruin it all? He's already ruined my life."

"God Almighty, leave it go, Hope. Forget what happened. That was a long time ago. You never go out, you never do anything, you never want to see anyone."

"Look at me! You think I like people seeing me like this? You think I like people staring while I hobble around like an old woman? Like some kind of freak! Morgan did this to me. And I'm never going to forgive him for it."

"It was an accident. You're his sister, he loves you. How many times does he have to ask you to forgive him?"

"I don't give a damn. Let's see him spend the rest of his life like this."

Booth shook his head and stared down, exhausted. He had heard all this before—time after time, after time—the hatred that was never going to fade, and growing more poisonous. He hurried across the sitting room and out the front screen door. By the time Hope had hobbled out onto the covered porch, Booth had gotten in his truck and was driving away. Hope went to the far end of the porch and watched the truck race up the road towards the mine.

"I'll never forgive him," Hope said softly.

She looked further up the hill to the mine. The galvanized roofs of the deserted buildings were casting off rolling waves of heat, and she could faintly hear the low rumble of the mine shaft fans, and the heavy throbbing of the giant water pumps. It was a slow, heavy heartbeat as the water was brought to the surface and spit out into the foul smelling drainage ditches. The towering chimneys of the boiler house streamed ribbons of smoke, and the dominating outline of the mine resembled a threatening volcano.

———————————

Addison Chase sat at his large mahogany desk, dressed in a finely tailored black suit, tie and vest. He patiently read and initialed the latest mining reports which set before him in two orderly stacks. His fountain pen scratched hastily across the bottom of some of the reports. The ceiling fan revolved slowly and silently above him, keeping the drab office cool and comfortable.

There was a gentle knock on the door. "Yes?" said Addison without looking up.

The door opened and Jeffers, the head clerk stepped in. "Mr. Chase, Judge Gits would like to see you."

"In with him," replied Addison.

Jeffers opened the door wide and Judge Cyrus Gits swept past him, puffing on a thick black cigar, and leaving a trail of blue smoke behind.

Gits was short and rotund, and had a jolly-looking face, highlighted by snow-white hair and moustache; it was the cheerful face of a man who liked people—enjoyed talking with them—enjoyed manipulating them. His flashy clothes were as bright as his smile. He wore a white fedora hat with a wide, brown band around the crown, and his brown checkered suit was set off by an equally white vest with gold buttons. The handle of his ivory walking stick was also of gold. His shoes shone as if made of glass.

Addison smiled and stood up, extending his hand. "Cyrus."

"Addison, my boy," replied Gits, eagerly shaking hands. "You look more like your father every time I see you."

"Sit, Cyrus. What can I do for you?"

"First, how's that wonderful mother of yours?"

"Irascible as ever."

Gits gave a low, growling laugh. "Good, good," he said, then grew serious. He took a puff on his cigar before he spoke. "This situation at mine seven, how serious is it?"

"Not very."

"The only reason I ask is, a lot of the merchants in town are very apprehensive. If this becomes a long strike, it could hurt the economy of Palmyra. There's three hundred and fifty miners out there, plus their women, and endless broods of brats. If the strike goes long…"

"It won't," said Addison confidently. "Besides, there are lots of other mines in the coal field, Cyrus."

"Yes, but we also have to think about getting bad newspaper coverage on this. Palmyra is growing, getting bigger every year. If the newspapers start slinging mud at Harwick Coal, or this town, well…"

"I wouldn't worry, Cyrus. With enough money in the right places, we can get any newspaper in the state on our side. Especially if they think we're fighting a Red union conspiracy."

"Biggs, over at the Palmyra Times, asked about sending a reporter out there to talk with the miners."

"What did you say?"

"That it wouldn't be in his best interests. Brewster would frown on it."

"You did right, Cyrus."

Gits smiled and glanced around the desk for an ash tray. Addison shoved a stack of reports to the edge of the desk, and Gits tapped a blobbed of gray ash onto the top page.

"Is Brewster busting a gut over this thing yet?" asked Gits.

"He's not happy."

Gits laughed, then sobered. "I hope this won't turn into an ugly battle. We both know Brewster has the appetite of a wolf."

"I can handle Brewster."

"But if the strikers won't knuckle under…"

"They will."

"You sure?" There was deep concern in Gits' expression.

Addison nodded reassuringly. "There's so much coal on the market right now that the loss of production from one mine doesn't matter. And I spoke to Zweig, at mine seven's company store. He says there's only enough food in stock for thirty days."

"So?"

"If the miners don't go back to work, we'll seal off the mine area. No one goes in or out. How long do you think they'll be able to last with no food and no money?"

"Good. The sentiment on the street is either get these people back to work, or get rid of them. I'll sign whatever injunctions or warrants you need. Just tell me how many."

"I don't think there'll be any need for that. This strike will fizzle like a damp match."

"But if it spreads to the other mines in the field? You know how this riff-raff sticks together."

"You're worrying about nothing, Cyrus."

"Excellent. That's what I wanted to hear," said Gits, getting up.

Addison came around the desk and took him by the arm. "Tell everyone to continue on as usual," he said, escorting Gits to the door.

"I see you've got two deputies outside the front of the building," said Gits.

"And two at the back," said Addison.

"Expecting trouble?"

"That's up to the miners. I've got nothing but time on my side."

Gits stopped and turned to Addison. "Just when the hell are you going to get married and start a family? All you do is work. Exactly like your father. He died slaving away for Harwick Coal."

"What woman would have me? I work fourteen hours a day, go to bed, get up and go back to work. But I love it."

"I don't know," grumbled Gits, shaking his head. "You need to…"

"I'll let you know how things are going at mine seven," said Addison, opening the door. "Just spread the word the situation is well in hand; that Addison Chase guarantees it."

A worn-out, dusty four-door Dodge sedan drove to the curb, not far from the front doors of the Harwick Coal Company building. The black paint was faded, and the windshield had a long, jagged crack in it. The fenders were dented and covered with scratches.

Tom Mitchell got out of the driver's seat, Morgan McAlister from the front passenger seat, and Dan Ketchum and Kelly Pike from the rear seat. They were all clean shaven and dressed in their best shirt and trousers. The brims of their sweat-stained hats were bent low, shading their eyes from the blistering afternoon sun.

For a moment, they stood glancing at the busy activity of the town. Cars and trucks were moving up and down the main street; people were hurrying along the sidewalks or crossing the streets, talking and gesturing to one another. It felt good to be there—to see the clean wood and brick buildings, and the bright shiny glass of the store windows. It was a different world, and Morgan and the others enjoyed looking at it, smelling it; enjoyed the high spirits of the people who surrounded them, giving them a sense of relief their grim, daily existence. Yet the activity seemed also to mock them, and the life they had just left.

As the four approached the Harwick building, they saw two burly men get up out of wooden chairs beside the main doors. A deputy badge was pinned to their shirts, and each man wore a holster and revolver. The bill of their soft cloth caps almost touched their noses. The two men gave a cocky grin, and their right hands went to the revolver on their hip.

"You fellas lost?" asked the first deputy.

"You here to arrest us?" replied Morgan, unintimidated.

"Only if you start something."

"We'd like to see Mr. Chase," said Morgan.

"Well, what you want," said the first deputy, "and what you get are two entirely different things."

The second deputy stepped off the sidewalk and circled around behind Morgan and the others, his hand on his revolver. Pike turned to face him, unafraid. Ketchum put a hand on Pike's arm to warn him to stay calm.

"I'd appreciate it, if you'd tell Mr. Chase the strike committee from mine seven would like to speak with him."

"He's busy," said the deputy.

"We'll wait then," said Mitchell.

The deputy grunted. "It's a hot day, why don't you hard-noses go on over to the drug store and have a cherry phosphate with crushed ice, then run on home."

"We didn't come here to go to the drug store," said Morgan.

"I already told you, Mr. Chase is busy," replied the deputy, taking a step forward.

"Hey," said the other deputy roughly. "Leave now or go sit in a jail cell. And it'll be a long sit."

Ketchum came up beside Morgan and spoke softly. "We better go, this ain't working."

"Your cracker-box of a jail don't scare me," said Pike, his eyes on the deputy in the street. They stared with obvious contempt for one another.

"Can't do much from behind iron bars," said Mitchell quietly to Morgan. "God only knows when they'd let us out."

Morgan thought a moment. "Tell Mr. Chase we'll be back."

"Not in this life time, striker," answered the first deputy.

Morgan and the others returned to their car.

"Now what?" asked Ketchum, wiping sweat from his face.

"The hell with Chase," said Pike. "Harwick's out at his goddamn castle, let's…"

"There'll be guards there too," said Mitchell. "Probably three times as many."

"Tom's right," said Morgan. "They want to play hardball, we'll play hardball."

"What do you mean?" asked Ketchum.

"They got guards, we'll have guards. Nobody goes in or out of the mine without our say so."

"Armed guards," said Pike.

"No," said Morgan quickly. "No guns."

"We've still got to get Chase to talk to us," said Mitchell.

"He'll talk," replied Morgan. "Our mine has the best coal in the entire field. And that means money. Money they ain't getting."

The four got back into the car. Mitchell made a U-turn in the wide main street, and they saw Sheriff Deets leaning against a mail box, on the corner, watching. He lit a cigarette, smiled, and waved his hand.

Isabel Chase sat stiffly at the large round dining table, dressed in an emerald green satin dress, a long double strand of pearls flowing down the front. The elegant drape of the sleeves hung over the arms of her chair. Her silver hair was brushed back away from her face, giving her an almost mannish appearance. But no one could mistake the regal presence of a "queen bee". With knife and fork, she sliced the broiled chicken breast in thin slices then took a sip of wine from her long-stemmed goblet. She turned when she heard the front door open and close. She listened to the approaching footsteps.

"Why, Addison," she said, "I didn't know you'd be home for lunch."

"I can't stay long," replied Addison, taking off his suit coat and hanging it on the back of the chair, across from Isabel. He sat down, undid a few buttons of his vest, and loosened his tie.

Isabel picked up a small crystal bell and jiggled it sharply. Its piercing tone resounded off the richly styled Victorian paneling and dark tapestries. The suddenness of the bell caused Addison to flinch then he rested his elbows on the table and began massaging his forehead. The deep shadows of the large, high-ceiled room created a gloomy atmosphere, and a tall grandfather clock, against one of the walls, ticked loudly, dominatingly.

Elinor, the maid, rushed from a door on the far side of the room, her sky-blue uniform and white apron creating the only bright colors anywhere.

"Elinor," began Isabel, "have cook fix Mr. Addison a chicken breast and…"

"No," interrupted Addison. "I don't have time. Just bring me a cheese sandwich and glass of cold milk, please."

"Yes, sir," said Elinor, scurrying back across the room.

Isabel studied Addison a moment as he continued rubbing his forehead. "You don't look good, Addison. You can't stay well if you don't eat right."

"I'm not hungry," said Addison, sitting back in his chair.

"Why do you have to wolf down a sandwich and rush back to work? You'll make yourself sick."

"I'm not going back to the office. I have to be at Brewster's at one o'clock. He called before I left the office and…"

"God, I hate it when he comes here for the summer," said Isabel, grabbing her napkin from her lap and throwing it on the table. "He parades around like he's just descended from the clouds of Olympus."

Addison smiled tiredly. "Yes, but he's still the boss, mother."

"When he inherited Harwick Coal, he should have made you a partner, not just the president."

"I like my job."

"You work too hard."

"Because I love to. I love the work. I love the money. Just like father did."

"And he worked himself into the grave; slaving away for Brewster's father, like you're slaving away for the son. Your father dropped dead from a stroke in the very office you're in."

"Well, hopefully, I have a few more years left yet," said Addison flippantly.

Elinor rushed into the room carrying a large plate with a small cheese sandwich, and tall glass of milk. She set it down gently in front of Addison.

"Thank you, Elinor."

"The milk's nice and cold, Mr. Addison, just like you like it."

"You're an angel."

Elinor giggled. "Cook just made some fresh sugar cookies, would you…"

"Elinor?" said Isabel sternly.

"Yes, ma'am?"

"Go."

"Yes, ma'am."

As Addison nibbled at his sandwich, Isabel pushed her plate away, no longer interested in her lunch.

"You were a sickly child, Addison. I nursed you through one illness after another. I don't want to see you go through that again."

"Thank you, mother. The cheese will make me strong," said Addison jokingly, and took a large bite of his sandwich.

"This is nothing to joke about. Don't ruin yourself over that man. You should be where he is. You're more intelligent than he'll ever be."

Addison dropped his sandwich onto his plate and looked across the table. "If it wasn't for Brewster, I wouldn't even be president of Harwich Coal. He handed me the job soon as I came out of college."

"Because he was too busy drinking and whoring to run his father's empire. It wasn't because he liked you."

Addison took a long swallow of milk, set the glass down and stared at the table. Isabel waited for him to say something, then:

"I don't want you to spend your life following orders and licking his boots. Your father did that with his father. Brewster is coarse and rude, and eats like a pig at the trough."

"What do you want me to do, slit his throat?"

"You've become too complacent. You're not moving ahead. You need more ambition."

"Judge Gits says I should start working less and get married; have a family."

"Gits? That senile rum-hound," said Isabel with contempt. "You'll have plenty of time later to find someone and get married."

"Yes, later. Later I'll find true love, and the perfect woman."

"Love is highly overrated. As are the women you think will provide it."

Addison got up. "I've got to go, Brewster will be waiting."

"Wait," said Isabel forcefully. "This miners' strike. If you don't end it soon Brewster will think you're weak. Don't let a bunch of low class ignorants make a fool out of you."

"I assure you that won't happen, mother," replied Addison, taking his suit coat from the back of the chair. "Elinor," he called.

Isabel grabbed the crystal bell and rang it violently.

Elinor appeared from behind the far door and stood practically at attention. "Yes, Mrs. Chase?"

"I'm ready to leave, Elinor," said Addison. "Please have Finch bring the car around."

"Yes, Mr. Addison.," replied Elinor, disappearing quickly.

Addison walked out of the room with Isabel following. They paused at the front doors of the entrance hall. Isabel helped Addison on with his coat, smoothed the lapels, buttoned his vest, and straightened his tie. She smiled and gave him a kiss on the cheek.

Addison smiled back, picking up his hat from the table beside the doors. "I'll try and be home on time for dinner."

"I'll wait."

"Please don't"

Addison's chauffeured car drove up at the foot of the long stone stairway leading down from the wide front porch. Addison opened the door and started out.

"What about those people out there?" asked Isabel.

"The deputies?"

"They make me nervous. And they're leaving footprints all over the lawns and gardens."

"They're just a precaution against the miners. They won't be here long."

"I hope not."

"It'll all be over soon. Not to worry."

Addison and Isabel kissed each other on the cheek, and he hurried across the porch and down the steps to where the chauffeur stood with the rear passenger door open.

"And don't let Brewster bully you," called Isabel.

Addison gave a quick wave and got into the car. Isabel watched it speed away. Her eyes and face were set in a hard, dark look. "You have just as much power as he does," she said quietly.

———————

Brewster Harwick was seated at his end of the sixteen-foot dining table reading a newspaper and finishing his lunch of broiled lamb chops. He was dressed in a coarse black shirt and trousers, and his dark-brown hunting hat was hanging from the corner knob of his high-backed chair. At the other end of the table sat Abigail Harwick, his magnificent young wife. Her form-fitting, pale yellow silk dress clung to her with darker bands of narrow yellow ribbon emphasizing her firm figure even more. There were several gold bracelets on each wrist, reflecting a soft light towards her deep green eyes. Her fire-red hair shone like the silk of her dress.

Abigail delicately cut into the lamb chop on her plate as she kept her eyes on Brewster, who was still absorbed in his newspaper, and chewing noisily on a mouthful of lamb.

"Is that the paper from Chicago?" asked Abigail.

"Yes," said Brewster, reading.

"I'd like to see it when you're done."

Brewster took another bite of his chop then threw the bone down. "Do these seem dry to you?"

"You had to devour four of them before you realized that?" said Abigail, taking a small bite of lamb from her fork.

Suddenly there was a muted, rapid thumping above them. Brewster looked at the ceiling. "What the hell's that?"

"I suspect it's the children playing. Nanny already fed them."

"Can't they play outside?"

"It's cooler in the house. Besides, those men walking around out there scare them with those guns."

That was Addison's idea. Incase the miners get out of hand. I approve."

"I don't."

Brewster ignored her and continued reading.

"Do we have to stay here the entire summer, like last year?"

"Yes."

"There's nothing to do, and the children really can't tolerate the heat and humidity."

"They'll get used to it."

"And I'm bored already."

"Go into Palmyra. Look around. Buy something."

"What? A sack of coal? A bushel of turnips?"

Brewster finally looked at her. "This is my vacation. I come here to relax—enjoy myself."

"And I enjoy Chicago. There's the theater, restaurants, dinner parties. It's very unboring."

"I'm not bored."

"I am."

"Get over it; we're staying."

Abigail shoved her plate halfway down the table in Brewster's direction, but he gave no reaction and went back to the newspaper.

The muted, rapid thumping began again in the ceiling, and Brewster jerked his head up. "What the hell are they doing now?"

"They're two young children trying to have some fun. Like I would."

"Then go upstairs and play with them."

Abigail shoved her chair back and stood up. "And what if they were two sons, not two daughters? Would it be all right for them to stomp around and holler?"

"Sons? Yes, it would," replied Brewster staring at the newspaper.

"Well, if you want sons, you can give birth to them. I'm not going through that hell again."

Brewster looked up, resentment in his eyes. "You were adequately compensated."

Abigail left the room, slamming the tall hand carved door behind her.

"You forgot your newspaper," yelled Brewster, mashed it into a jagged ball and threw it to the far end of the table. He then picked up the half-eaten lamb chop from his plate and chewed angrily.

There was a delicate knock on the door Abigail had gone out of.

"What?" shouted Brewster.

The door opened and the head of Myra, the maid, came into view. "Mr. Brewster, Mr. Addison and Sheriff Deets are here," she said meekly.

"Bring them in," replied Brewster with a wave of his hand, and slumped back in his chair.

After a few moments, the door opened again and Addison came in, hat in hand, followed by Deets, hat in hand.

"Sit," said Brewster, motioning to two chairs to the right of the long table.

Deets sat quickly, clutching his hat in both hands. Addison set his hat on the table and took off his coat, draping it over the back of his chair.

"I hope you don't mind, Brewster," said Addison, "the drive over was a little warm."

"Fine. Sit."

"When I came in I saw Abigail going up the stairs," said Addison, making himself comfortable in his chair. "Sorry I didn't get a chance to speak with her."

"Lucky you," said Brewster.

"And how are the children? I'd like to see…"

"I didn't call this meeting to talk about my domestic life," interrupted Brewster.

Addison smiled, ignoring Brewster's usual gruffness, and said, "Then let's get on with it."

"Deets," began Brewster, picking up a solid gold toothpick from beside his plate, and beginning to pick his teeth.

"Yes, sir?"

"Mr. Addison informed me you went to mine seven, and served the eviction notice."

"Absolutely, Mr. Harwick."

"And?"

Deets stared at Harwick a moment, then at Addison, giving himself time to think. He knew what was coming.

"Just how many miners have moved?" asked Brewster ominously.

"Well, you see, Mr. Harwick," began Deets.

"Addison," said Brewster, "how many?"

"None that I know of."

"None," said Brewster, looking straight at Deets. "No miners moved out; no coal moved out."

"Brewster, we agreed to wait this out," said Addison. "Let the miners wear themselves…"

"I'm not waiting till Hell freezes over," said Brewster loudly

"They're out of work," said Addison, "and they'll soon be out of money.

"And so will I," shouted Brewster.

Deets flinched at the loud words as they reverberated around the high-ceiled room, and looked to Addison, who simply shrugged at the ludicrous remark.

"Don't," said Brewster, pointing at Addison, "don't dare shrug this off. I've waited all I'm going to wait."

"It's only been six days," began Addison, "what..."

"I'm not going to wait six more hours," said Brewster, pounding the table.

"Then what do you want to do?" asked Addison calmly.

"I want Deets, here, to start arresting people; get them off company property. I want new miners brought in."

"It's not that simple," replied Addison.

"Yes, it is," snapped Brewster. "Deets you're the law here in this county, aren't you?"

"Yes, but..."

"I thought maybe you'd forgotten that."

"There's only so much I can do with those people," said Deets anxiously. "If this turns serious, I'm going to need a lot of armed deputies to..."

"It's already turned serious," said Brewster angrily. "Where the hell have you been?"

Deets avoided Brewster's hostile gaze, glanced at Addison, hoping for help, but got none.

"I want every mine, in my coal field, running at capacity. If production slows down the coal buyers, in all the big cities, will go elsewhere to buy coal. And I don't intend to lose that kind of money."

"But it's only one mine," said Deets. "Out of..."

"Shut up, Deets," yelled Brewster.

"Sorry, sir."

"Deets?"

"Yes, sir?"

"I'm negotiating for a seventy thousand acre coal field in Pennsylvania, and a forty thousand acre coal field in Kentucky, and that takes money. If my mines here aren't producing, there's no money to buy other coal fields, is there?"

"No, Mr. Harwick."

"It takes millions of dollars, Deets. Have you ever seen millions of dollars?"

Deets shook his head slowly, having absolutely no idea what that amount of money would look like.

"Well, I have," said Brewster, getting up. "And I want to see a lot more of it. And so, gentlemen, I expect you to go out and do your jobs. Now I have to take a bath, and go horseback riding. I'm supposed to be on vacation. But you'd never know it!" The last five words came in a savage shout.

Deets stared down, intimidated by Brewster's anger, but Addison just examined his clean, buffed fingernails, refusing to be baited into an argument.

Brewster shoved his chair back with a quick jerked of his legs and started across the room. "Hire as many goons as you need," he said to Deets. "But get those miners out." He stopped and stared hard at Deets. "And if there are any union organizers involved with those miners, I want to know about it right away."

"I haven't heard of any union…"

"What do you hear?" said Brewster sarcastically, and stalked out of the room.

Deets and Addison sat quietly for a moment, then looked at one another.

"Well," said Addison, "so much for diplomacy."

"What?"

"Nothing," said Addison, getting up.

Deets stood quickly, saying, "Mr. Chase, I know quite a few of those miners out there. A lot of them can't read or write, but they make up for it in toughness, and stubbornness. There's at least three hundred of them, and…"

"Three hundred and fifty."

"And every one of them has a gun."

"And you're the sheriff," said Addison, putting on his coat.

"And I'd like to remain a live sheriff."

Addison put on his hat, looked at Deets, and gave a resigned gesture with his hands. "The great god Harwick has spoken. Do what you've been ordered." Addison walked away.

"I'll need more deputies," said Deets pleadingly.

"Hire them," said Addison without turning. "The money will be provided."

Deets remained where he was, staring at nothing, and shaking his head. "Holy Christ," he whispered.

CHAPTER 3

The sun had barely risen, but the air was already warm and the wind dead. Five cars, their tops folded down, were racing up the dusty road leading into the housing area of mine seven. Sheriff Deets was in the lead car with three deputies; the other cars that followed each carried four deputies.

Dogs began barking and chickens clucked frantically and flapped their wings to get out of the way of the speeding cars. Peoples' faces began appearing at the windows and screen doors. The engines of the five vehicles shattered the quiet morning calm. When Deets and his deputies reached the far end of the main street, two cars pulled to the left, two to the right; the fifth stopped in the middle of the road, where four deputies got out, their pump shotguns at the ready.

Deets and his other men sprang from their cars, one group assailing a house on the right side of the street, and the other group a house on the left side of the street. Screaming and yelling could be heard. Children began crying, then there was the angry voices of men and women. Deputies began hurling furniture out the front doors, then windows were smashed as tables and chairs were thrown out; next came clothing, and pots and pans.

Women and children ran from the two houses, their hands over their heads to protect themselves—they were terrified, and still half asleep. The men of the houses were dragged out onto the porches and thrown down the steps. It wasn't long before a crowd began to gather; first a few came running, then more and more.

Tom Mitchell appeared at the edge of the crowd dressed only in trousers, and barefooted and barechested. He turned to a small girl beside him, saying, "Get Morgan, quick."

The girl ran off as fast as she could.

Dan Ketchum joined the growing mob, his shirt still unbuttoned and his trousers hanging loose at the end of his suspenders. He watched the deputies heave more possessions out the windows and doors of the two homes. He turned to a lanky, freckle-faced boy, and whispered, "Tell, Pike. Run."

The boy shoved his way out of the crowd and ran.

The groups of men were growing agitated at what they were seeing; the women and children afraid. Tom Mitchell worked his way across the crowd to where Deets stood on the porch of one of the homes, his hand on his holstered revolver, his eyes studying the hostile people still filling the street.

"Curtis," called Mitchell, "what the hell are you doing?"

"You were warned to get out," replied Deets loudly. "Now you're going! And you can take your strike with you! Chase and Harwick don't need you. Won't be long a trainload of niggers will be coming in to replace you."

A sound went through the crowd; not so much a moan, but a threatening reply. Deets couldn't help gripping his revolver tighter.

"Who the hell are you to come in here and bust up our homes?" shouted a miner.

"I'm the law," Deets yelled. "You're breaking the law, and you'll be punished by the law!"

"Go back to Palmyra, you old windbag," cried one of the women.

There was laughter and shouts of agreement.

"I noticed," called out a miner, "that when you piss on a fire it keeps burning."

There was more laughter and derisive cat-calls. Deets's face turned beet-red and he didn't know what to do.

"Hey, Deets," shouted another voice, "you're about as welcome here as General Sherman marching through Georgia."

The men and women applauded, and the children grinned and jumped up and down, happy that the fear was leaving them.

Morgan McAlister worked his way through the mob, his face heavy with anxiety. Katherine was close behind him, then held back when Morgan approached Deets.

"Chase send you here?" asked Morgan.

"And Harwick himself," answered Deets. "You people are done."

"This may be Wapakonetka County, but it's still the United States of America," said Morgan.

"What the hell's that supposed to mean?" asked Deets.

"These are our homes, you can't kick us out like we're nobody; nothing."

"If you didn't want trouble, you should have kept your mouths shut, and your bodies working," replied Deets.

"Who are you to tell us to move on?" shouted a miner. "Where we going to go? Where we going to find work?"

"You should of thought of that before this," said Deets. "You dumb plow mules!"

The crowd groaned and surged forward. Deets and his deputies aimed their weapons.

Morgan raised his arms, yelling, "Stay back, stay back."

The crowd relaxed, and Morgan turned to Deets, taking a few paces towards him.

"Beating people, throwing them out of their homes ain't the law," said Morgan calmly.

"It is now," replied Deets, sweat streaming down his face.

"And if we don't leave," said Morgan, "you going to burn us out?"

"Do I have to?"

Morgan took a moment to calm himself, then spoke. "You have access to Chase and Harwick, ask them to talk to us; if not to me, then to whoever they choose. It doesn't…"

Deets grunted, and said, "You people are doomed. Give up and go back to work."

"Why the hell should we let you scare us into going back to work?" shouted a miner.

"Because I've got the law on my side," Deets shouted back. "What the hell do you have?"

"We got guns," answered a loud voice.

Morgan and the crowd turned and looked up the street. Kelly Pike, and thirty armed miners, came towards them. They were grim-faced and ready for a fight—ready to kill or die—and showing no fear. Pike and his group gathered around Morgan, and stood staring at Deets and his nervous deputies.

"I guess it's time we all oiled up our guns, boys," yelled a miner, far back in the huge crowd.

A deafening cheer went up.

"You people are trespassing," shouted Deets, barely audible. "You can get sixty days in jail for vagrancy; and when that's up another sixty days for defying the law!"

"Haw…haw…haw!" came a derisive, mule-braying voice from one of Pike's group.

Everyone began laughing again, and Morgan walked up closer to Deets.

"Curtis," said Morgan in a friendly tone, "I think you better leave."

Deets stared at Morgan a moment then glanced at the guns held by Pike's men, and the hundreds of undaunted, hostile faces.

"What good is going to come from any violence," said Morgan softly.

"I come here to see justice is served," said Deets half-heartedly.

"And what about charity?" said Morgan.

Deets' defiant eyes dropped for a moment then went back to Morgan.

"Chase and Harwick fill their pockets, and reward all their greedy, corrupt friends by the sweat of our brow," said Morgan. "And they believe they're doing us a favor by paying us seven dollars and fifty cents a day. This is a battle for survival. It ain't a matter of picking up and moving on."

Deets hesitated, not knowing what to say, then walked down the steps of the porch, his deputies following. The deputies on the opposite side of the street also moved to their cars.

Silently the sea of people parted, and watched the five vehicles drive in a line up the street, and out of the housing area.

All eyes then went to Morgan. He walked to the nearest house that had been ransacked, and stood on the porch, facing the crowd.

"All right," said Morgan loudly, "now we know what we're up against. We can go back to work, or go on and finish this, no matter what."

"Finish it," shouted voice after voice.

Morgan's gaze swept the eager faces and waving fists, and made his decision. "This mine is ours," he yelled. "And these houses are ours! And we'll give it all back when we get what we want!"

A thunderous cry went up, and reached far above the mine itself, carrying over beyond the surrounding hills—a cry of triumph.

"Put up the barricades," shouted Morgan, and his words were drowned out in another cheer.

Morgan came down the steps of the porch as Tom Mitchell walked up, saying, "We should have done this in the beginning."

"I was hoping it wouldn't come to this, Tom."

"No turning back now."

"Take as many men as you need and secure the mine," ordered Morgan. "We can't have anything happening to it."

"Good as done," said Mitchell, walking away, shouting out names of the men he would need.

"Dan Ketchum," called Morgan, "where are you?"

"Here, Morgan," answered Ketchum, coming out of the milling swarm.

Morgan put a hand on his shoulder. "I want you to post lookouts all around the mine, and all the roads in and out of here."

"Done," said Ketchum, hurrying off.

"And put some men on the well pump," Morgan added. "We have to keep the water supply safe."

Ketchum waved a hand in acknowledgement.

Morgan turned to go as Kelly Pike came towards him, his rifle cradled in his arm. They stared at one another.

"I know, don't say it," said Pike.

"You couldn't leave the guns at home, could you?" said Morgan with a disapproving shake of his head.

"And let Deets get away with what he was trying?" replied Pike. "Besides, he's just another goon on a leash. Chase and Harwick are out to destroy us."

"Then don't help them," said Morgan. "I don't need any hotheads running this strike. I'm in charge. If you don't like it then vote me out."

"No," said Pike contritely. "No, I'm not against you, I…"

"Then don't do this again."

"You're the mine boss, tell us what to do."

Morgan gave Pike a friendly pat on the back, saying, "You and those other young bucks pull up a couple sections of railroad tracks. I don't want any trains coming in or out until I say so."

Pike smiled. "I like it."

"One more thing," said Morgan. "Until I say otherwise, I don't want anybody walking around with a loaded gun."

"What?"

"Keep the cartridges in your pockets."

"But what…"

"Those are my orders, Kelly."

"Fine," replied Pike half-heartedly. "I'll tell the men."

———————

There was a gentle knock on the front screen door of Booth McAlister's house. A few seconds later Booth came to the door and saw Morgan standing there.

"I need to talk to you," said Morgan in a troubled tone.

"Sure. Come on in."

"We can talk out here."

"No, no," said Booth, opening the screen door. "It's cooler in here."

Morgan hesitated then entered, but stood just inside the room, looking around.

"Hope is out back," said Booth, sensing Morgan's uneasiness. "She's watering her roses. Don't know why. They don't grow worth a damn."

"Deets and his deputies just tried to run us off."

"I heard. I was up at the mine checking things or I'd have been there with you."

"Wouldn't have done any good."

Booth motioned to a chair. "Go on, sit."

"No, I can't stay long."

"Sit. You're always welcome here, any time."

Morgan took a seat and so did Booth. There was an awkward silence for a few moments.

"We're sealing off the mine and the housing area," began Morgan. "We can't let Deets back in."

"Chase won't stand for it," replied Booth.

"We know. If you and Hope want to leave just say the word. I don't expect you two to go through this with us."

"This is my mine as much as it is yours. I can't leave, and I won't side with you. I'd be blacklisted just like you and the others will be."

"This could be a long, hungry strike, Booth. I think you should go."

"Part of my job is to protect all this property here."

"We intend to keep control until Chase or Harwick knuckle under."

Booth simply shook his head.

"Is Hope prepared to go through this with you?" asked Morgan. "Maybe you could put her up at the hotel in Palmyra."

"She won't go. Especially if she knows it's your idea."

Morgan stared down a moment. "We…we never were much of a family, I guess. Even from the beginning. Ma dying young, and pa drinking himself to death over it. Then Hope gets hurt and…" Morgan stopped and shrugged. "She just won't listen when I try talking to her."

"The hate's gone too deep," said Booth. "There's nothing you can say or do."

"I think about that day a lot," said Morgan. "The three of us; just snot-nosed kids. Stole old man Finney's two-seater roadster just to go for a wild ride—a joy ride they call it. Funny, things would have turned out a lot different, if I hadn't of been driving fast, or that front tire hadn't of blown out. I still remember the noise that old car made rolling over and over down the embankment—and Hope screaming. And me and you never got a scratch. Why'd it have to be Hope?"

"Won't do any good to keep reliving it, Morgan. Let it go. Nothing's going to change. Hope's a different person now. She's not the sister we knew before."

Morgan looked at Booth and smiled. "You're a damn fine brother. Always have been. Better than me."

"Wish I could help you, Morgan, but I can't."

Morgan nodded. "I still think you and Hope should go out of here."

"I've talked to the superintendents' of some of the other mines around here," said Booth. "They say their miners aren't going to support you in this. They're too afraid of losing their jobs. They need money more than they need a union."

"This isn't about unionizing; it's about changing this life we're living."

"Yeah," said Booth sadly, "coal mining's a hell of a way to make a dollar."

"Ain't that God's truth."

"If this strike turns violent, Morgan…"

"It can't. I won't let it. I need you to help me."

"I told you, I…"

"You can get to Chase. Ask him…"

"Holy Christ, Morgan," said Booth, getting up and pacing across the room, "to Chase and Harwick we've got no more worth than a herd of sheep. They live in another world. What we make in a year, they spend in a week."

"Thanks to our sweat and blood, and maimed bodies."

"So what?" said Booth angrily, continuing to pace the room. "You're not going to change anything."

"We've got to try. No matter what."

The kitchen screen door banged shut and Hope called out Booth's name.

"In here," replied Booth.

Morgan got up as Hope came to the doorway of the kitchen, leaning heavily on her canes.

"You should see my roses, they're starting to…" Hope saw Morgan, and her smile was quickly replaced with hostile eyes.

"Hello, Hope," said Morgan gently.

"Morgan stopped by to say 'hi'," said Booth. "You have any more of that ice tea left?"

"No," said Hope, staring coldly at Morgan.

"We'll talk later, Booth," said Morgan walking towards the front screen door.

"This mine don't belong to you and those miners," Hope blurted out.

"Hope," said Booth warningly.

"And it never will," she added.

"Leave it be," said Booth.

"The hell I will," replied Hope. "He ruins everything he gets near."

Booth followed Morgan out onto the front porch. "Morgan, wait."

Morgan turned.

"Whatever happens," continued Booth, "you'll always be my brother. No matter what Hope says, or feels, that's her, not me."

Morgan and Booth stood looking at one another, they wanted to hug each other, but instead grasped hands tightly.

"Good luck," said Booth.

"And you," said Morgan, turning and walking quickly away.

Hope appeared at the screen door. "Why'd you let him in here?"

Booth's shoulders slumped, and he moved with a tired gait towards his truck. "I'll be up at the mine."

"Why?" asked Hope. "It don't belong to you, you let Morgan take it away."

In the outer office of Addison Chase's office, the clerks were busy at their desks typing, talking on telephones, and replacing and retrieving letters and mining reports from the tall oak filing cabinets occupying and entire back wall.

Near the main entrance, sitting on a narrow wooden bench was a meek looking little man with a pale, bony face, and slender hooked nose. His hair was short and wiry, almost gray—same as his bushy eyebrows. He was dressed all in black and gripped a black derby hat in one hand, and a thin leather briefcase in the other. He kept staring at the door to Addison Chase's office. After a few minutes he got up and crossed to the waist-high railing separating the waiting area from the clerk's area.

"Excuse me," said the man softly.

No one paid any attention. He waited, then realized he was being ignored. "Excuse me," he said loudly.

Jeffers, the head clerk, looked up from his desk, saying, "Yes, what is it?"

"I've been waiting for over an hour," began the man. "I need to see Mr..."

"Mr. Chase is very busy. If you want to make an appointment, perhaps he'll see you tomorrow," said Jeffers.

"But I came all the way from Columbus. I need to speak personally with Mr. Chase."

"Where are you staying?" asked Jeffers with a tired sigh.

"The Palmyra House."

"I'll have Mr. Chase phone you there."

"When?"

Jeffers glared at the annoying little man a moment, then forced a thin smile to his dry lips. "Earlier you said you had a report to give Mr. Chase."

"Yes. Concerning mine seven. It's very..."

"Well, give it to me, and I'll see it's put on his desk," said Jeffers, holding out his hand.

The man clutched his briefcase tighter to his chest and shook his head. "I have give it to Mr. Chase personally."

Growing frustrated, Jeffers motioned to one of the clerks who hurried over and leaned down. "Sims," whispered Jeffers, "go down stairs and ask one of the deputies to..."

The main door to the office burst open and in swept Brewster Harwick dressed in a blinding white suit, vest, shirt, tie and hat, and shoes to match. A cigarette holder with smoldering cigarette was clenched between his teeth.

"Don't get up, I'm just slumming," said Brewster, jokingly, and crossed towards the door of Addison's office.

"Mr. Harwick, how wonderful to see you," said Jeffers, leaping out of his chair, looking as if he was about to drop to one knee and kiss Brewster's hand.

Brewster continued on to Addison's office.

"Is that Brewster Harwick himself?" asked the little man with the briefcase.

Jeffers waved him away.

Brewster pounded on the door of Addison's office, shouting, "Wake up, Addison, the boss is here."

The little man with the briefcase started in Brewster's direction, but Jeffers, and another clerk, cut him off.

Addison opened the door of his office. "Good, God," he said, "what are you doing here? Is the world coming to an end?"

"Worse," replied Brewster, leaning in the doorway. "Abigail wouldn't stop screeching till I brought her to town to buy out all the stores. Then she wants to go to one of those god-awful Hollywood movies. Luckily, I was able to escape. Hide me quick."

"Mr. Harwick, Mr. Chase," called the little man, and waved his derby in the air.

"Yes," Brewster called back, "nice to see you too," and took Addison by the arm and entered his office, slamming the door shut.

"Lord, I need a drink," said Brewster, moving to Addison's desk. "No, I need three or four. What do you have?"

"Ice water," replied Addison.

"What the hell's wrong with you?" asked Brewster, looking around the room. "You've enough space in here for your own saloon."

"Drinking on the job creates a bad impression."

"Not with me." Brewster moved to behind Addison's desk, ran his fingers over the back of the large padded leather chair. "Very plush, Addison. I approve." He swirled the chair around and dropped into it, and made himself comfortable. "Fits my ass perfectly."

"Be my guest," said Addison, seating himself in one of the wooden chairs on the far side of the desk. He studied Brewster a moment, then smiled. "What are you up to? You're in an awfully damn good mood."

"Believe it or not, I've taken some time to do some serious thinking."

"Praise, God, His wonders to behold."

"Don't be a facetious ass."

"And what great gem of wisdom have you come up with?"

"The way you want to handle mine seven. As much as I hate to admit it, you're right. Let them sit out there and starve. We can make up the loss of production by increasing production at the other mines. And no money is lost at all."

"That's what I've been saying from the start."

"Don't try and out think me, I don't like it."

Addison bowed his head. "Your decisions are always final, not mine."

"Yes," said Brewster, propping his feet up on the desk, and taking a quick drag on his cigarette holder. "You sure you don't have a little drop of bourbon squirreled away somewhere?"

Before Addison could answer, they heard loud voices in the outer office that soon turned into yelling. The door to Addison's office flew open, and the little man with the briefcase was struggling to get in as Jeffers clawed away at his coat, which was about to come off him.

"Mr. Harwick, Mr. Chase, I need to see you," pleaded the man.

"Who the hell are you?" asked Addison, suppressing a grin.

"Wilmer Turpin, Mr. Chase. Head geologist with the firm of Walsh, Wilde, and Plunkett. You hired us last spring."

"And you're just showing up now?" said Brewster with a loud laugh. "Fire him, Addison."

"No, no," said the man. "We've just finished our report, and it was imperative I speak with you personally."

"Imperative," said Brewster, looking at Addison with a raised eyebrow. "If it's imperative, it must be important."

Addison and Brewster couldn't help smiling as they watched the little man still struggling in the stranglehold of Jeffers arms.

"It's about our survey at mine seven," said the man.

The smiles faded quickly from Addison's and Brewster's faces.

"All right, Jeffers," said Addison with a wave of his hand.

Jeffers released Turpin, and with a hostile stare, went out, closing the door.

Turpin rushed to the desk, set his derby and briefcase down and nodded to Brewster, saying, "So nice to have the pleasure of meeting you Mr. Harwick."

"Yes, I know. And meeting Mr. Chase also."

"Of course," said Turpin, nodding to Addison. "We've talked on the telephone several times."

"We have?" said Addison surprised.

"Months ago. To tell you the survey was progressing nicely."

"Well, I'm off," said Brewster, getting up. "I need someplace more secure to hide."

"Please wait, Mr. Harwick," said Turpin. "I'm sure you'll want to hear this. Oh, absolutely sure."

"Absolutely," said Addison, shaking a finger at Brewster.

"Fine," said Brewster, "just don't bore me." He walked to an open window and sat on the ledge. He took the short piece of cigarette from its holder and dropped to towards the sidewalk below, watching its descent. "Well," he said," placing the cigarette holder in his coat pocket, and looking back to Turpin, "what's this wonderful revelation you have to bestow on us?"

"Something very exciting," replied Turpin, opening his briefcase and taking out a thick sheaf of neatly typed pages, and a folded map. "In April, we were asked to investigate a coal vein in one of mine seven's tunnels; per Mr. Chase's request."

"Oh, yes," said Addison, "now I remember."

"You were worried the vein was petering out."

"I don't find this interesting at all," said Brewster. "Please get to the point."

"What did you find?" asked Addison.

"The vein is definitely not petering out," said Turpin, his eyes wide, and with a grin from ear to ear. "We've named the new vein, the Colossal Vein."

Addison and Brewster glanced at one another, then Addison got out of his chair and faced Turpin, finally taking him seriously. Brewster moved from the window ledge to the leather chair at Addison's desk, sat down, and took off his hat.

"Why did you decide on that name?" asked Brewster.

Turpin's eyes and smile became wider. "Because that's what it is. We thought of Mammoth, Behemoth, Gigantic…"

"Fine, fine," said Brewster, annoyed. "What's in this report of yours?"

Turpin unfolded his map and smoothed it out on the desk. Addison and Brewster leaned in attentively. Turpin's finger began poking excitedly at the map.

"This new vein is roughly three miles wide and twenty miles long," began Turpin. "We estimate the shafts would be fourteen hundred to two thousand feet deep. Maybe more."

"Addison and Brewster looked at Turpin, wondering if he was insane, and this was all a joke.

"How sure are you?" asked Addison cautiously.

"Very sure, Mr. Chase."

Addison and Brewster threw a glance at one another.

"This could become the largest anthracite coal deposit in the entire world," said Turpin proudly.

"More than four hundred thousand tons a year?" asked Addison.

"Oh, much more than that," replied Turpin confidently. "Much, much more."

Brewster stared intently at the neatly drawn map in front of him. Addison, his mind reeling at the breath-taking prospects involved, sat down slowly in the wooden chair. He looked up at Turpin's grinning face, still wondering if he were a lair or lunatic.

Turpin continued, enjoying every second of his time in the limelight. "This new vein will employ thousands. And could be worked indefinitely." He placed the thick, typed report on top the map, stood up straight and threw his shoulders back. "Gentlemen, you're about to make history."

Addison stared at the map, his expression growing troubled, but Brewster rose from his chair, eyes on Turpin, and came around to the front of the desk. He grabbed Turpin in a powerful bear-hug, and began rocking him from side to side. Turpin began moaning, trying to break free.

Brewster stopped suddenly, nose to nose with Turpin. "I trust your office has said nothing about this to anyone else?"

"Of course not, sir. This is a confidential report. We wouldn't..."

"Excellent," said Brewster, releasing Turpin. "I'm very impressed with you Turpin. Imperatively impressed. Now you'll have to excuse us." Brewster led him towards the office door.

"Please," said Turpin, "my hat and briefcase."

"Hurry, Mr. Turpin, hurry," said Brewster as Turpin ran to the desk and snatched up his derby and briefcase.

Brewster put and arm around him and herded him towards the door again. "Now, Mr. Turpin, I want you and your associates at…at…"

"Walsh, Wilde, and Plunkett," said Turpin.

"Yes. Everyone there has to remain absolutely mum about all this."

"Oh, we don't discuss our clients' business with anyone, Mr. Harwick."

"Good. Keep it that way," said Brewster, opening the office door. "Thank you for stopping by."

"If you want us to do any more studies, on this vein, we can…"

"We'll call you," said Brewster, nudging Turpin out the door, and slamming it shut.

For a long moment, Addison and Brewster watched one another. Suddenly Brewster exploded into a wild jig that carried him across the room, and around to behind Addison's desk, where he flopped into the leather chair, all the while laughing and clapping.

"Settle down, Brewster," said Addison. "Settle down. We have to think this thing through."

"Think hell," shouted Brewster, slapping both hands on top the desk. "The Colossal Vein," he shouted. "Colossal!"

Brewster swiveled his chair around and stared out the window. "That coal field out there could become the greatest mining district in the world. My field. An inexhaustible supply of black diamonds." He sprang to his feet, yelling, "Brewster Harwick owns the world's greatest coal mine!"

"But it's all still very deep down in the ground, isn't it?" said Addison.

"Not for goddamn long, it isn't. I'll be richer than Andrew Carnegie ever was! Two hundred, three hundred million dollars right in my lap."

"But Mr. Carnegie gave most of his money away," said Addison, trying to bring Brewster back to reality.

"I know," said Brewster with a frown. "That's always bothered me. Why give away millions and millions? Something must have been eating at his conscience like a swarm of maggots."

"Or else he was a great humanitarian," said Addison, sarcastically.

"When the hell's the last time you ever met a rich son-of-a-bitch with the milk of human kindness in his veins?"

"You've got me there."

Brewster began circling Addison and the desk. "I want you to get hold of Garlow in Chicago."

"No, Brewster, not yet," said Addison, holding up his hands.

"Yes. That moron Deets hasn't been able to do anything right, so far."

"Give this mine seven thing a few more weeks."

"The hell I will. I want my coal! I want to see the Colossal Vein!"

"Garlow can be hard to control," said Addison. "Let's..."

"He settled the strike in Pennsylvania for us. And did it damn quick."

"If you like seeing a lot of blood, yes."

"Blood doesn't bother me. Call Garlow," said Brewster, walking to the office door.

"This won't be cheap," said Addison, getting up. "Lots of money, lots of food, whiskey, guns, tents..."

"Do it," said Brewster, opening the door and turning back. "The Colossal Vein will more than make up for the expenses. Besides, we need to start building more houses out there. You heard Mr. Turpin, we'll need thousands of miners, not hundreds."

Brewster stalked out and across the outer office, waving his hat, shouting, "Have a wonderful day, gentlemen."

The clerks all jumped to their feet, nodding and saying, "Thank you, Mr. Harwick, thank you."

Addison came to the doorway of his office, and stood looking after Brewster. It showed clearly on his face that he had no enthusiasm for what lay ahead. "Jeffers," he said calmly.

Jeffers rushed up. "Yes, Mr. Chase?"

"Get on the telephone. Try and locate Otis Garlow. Use whatever last number, or address you have for him."

"Is he the Mr. Garlow that was sent to Pennsylvania with his special police force?"

"Yes."

Jeffers thought a moment. "Then the mine seven strike has become serious, sir?"

Addison smiled weakly. "Not yet."

CHAPTER 4

It only took three days before a line of noisy, rolling boxcars—fifty in all—drew within view of mine seven. The powerful, steaming locomotive had been switched around at the Palmyra depot, and was pushing the long line of cars ahead of it at a slow speed. There were gangs of men sitting or lying on the roofs of the cars, others sitting and standing in the open doorways, looking towards the distant houses of the mine, and the mine buildings themselves.

The locomotive finally came to a stop with screeching wheels and a loud hiss of steam. Men began climbing down from the cars, stretching and talking and laughing. Their clothing was worn and shabby; their shoes scuffled and colorless, with soles paper-thin. All the faces were unshaven and dirty—faces with deep dark lines and jagged scars—ugly, leathery faces with no teeth, or one eye missing; emaciated faces full of hate and misery from long years of violence and cruelty.

The men moved away from the boxcars into an immense, flat area of few trees, tangled scrub brush, and dead, straw-colored grass. Some of the men walked with a limp or with cautious steps, suspicious of where they were. There were short, pig-faced men, tall scarecrow men, huge bear-shaped men, and lean, hungry looking men—cutthroats and loafers who had spent their lives breaking the law and running from it; now they were the law. Five hundred of them.

"All right, get with it," shouted an angry voice.

The gangs of men watched as Otis Garlow walked among them. He had the appearance of a God-fearing Amish farmer with his lean and muscular frame, and his long salt and pepper beard. His light gray eyes shone with excitement. But his soul was the Devil's own.

"Unload those cars," bellowed Garlow.

While the locomotive was unhitched, and began backing away down the tracks, the horde of men began tossing tents, blankets, and camping supplies out the doors of the boxcars. Cases of rifles and ammunition came next, then case after case of food goods.

Garlow moved swiftly through the camp area, shouting orders and pushing slow-movers out of his way.

Deets and three armed deputies entered the camp. Deets drove slowly through the frantic activity and rising clouds of dust.

"Where's Garlow?" Deets kept calling out, but the men only gave quick, distrustful glances at the shiny badges they saw and turned away. "Where's Garlow?" Deets yelled again.

"And who wants to know?" replied Garlow, approaching the car.

"I do," said Deets. "I'm the sheriff."

Grinning, Garlow looked Deets up and down. "You law dogs all look a like. Amazing."

"Don't get out of line, Garlow," said Deets, trying to put up a brave front in the midst of what he considered a swarming pack of mongrel dogs. "You're in Wapakoneta county now, not the slums of Chicago."

"There's a difference?" said Garlow, grinning and staring hard at Deets.

"Once you get your men settled, I've orders to deputize the lot of you," said Deets.

"Good. That way if we kill anyone it'll be legal, won't it?"

"You're here to force these miners back to work, or force them out," said Deets with obvious contempt. "Nothing more."

"Well, we sure as hell didn't come here to work in a goddamn coal mine," replied Garlow, and laughed loudly. "Addison Chase hired a special police force, and that's what he's getting."

"You don't look so special to me," said one of the deputies in the rear seat of the car.

Garlow took a few steps towards the deputy and held him in a chilling, dominating gaze. The deputy swallowed noticeably.

"What are they paying you, boy?" asked Garlow calmly.

"Four dollars a day."

Garlow laughed his big, deafening laugh, and said: "Boy, we're making ten dollars a day. So you see we *are* special. And what does that make you, law dog?"

The deputy turned his eyes away, and Garlow walked to the front of the car and stood surveying his campsite.

"Sheriff," he said, without turning, "after you swear in my men, we'll get to work. Understand?"

"You understand I'm the law here," said Deets.

"Mr. Chase hired us, not you," replied Garlow, and walked away.

"Holy Jesus," said the deputy seated next to Deets, "how in hell we going to control this bunch of scum?"

"We ain't, knothead, we ain't," said Deets, his eyes sweeping the area before him as the mobs of men began erecting tents of all sizes and shapes, and digging pits for camp fires.

A fistfight broke out, and men began gathering around, shouting and cheering—encouraging the fighters to do their worst to each other.

———————

The women and children of mine seven stood in scattered groups from one end of the housing area to the other, watching the distant activity of the growing campsite, and listening to the noises. The children were fascinated, but the women became filled with dread. They could see the hundreds of strikebreakers moving in what seemed like angry swarms; and their loud voices drifted in on the hot wind. Behind the thin, rising walls of dust could be seen the faint silhouettes of tents scattered in all directions.

At the community hall, Morgan McAlister stood on the high front porch at the front doors as all the miners assembled before him, agitated and resentful.

"All right, listen to me," said Morgan loudly. "We've all seen what's going on out there. And we know what it means."

"Dirty strikebreakers," yelled a man.

"Filthy scabs," yelled another.

"They're not coming in here," shouted more men.

A loud cry of agreement went up.

Morgan raised his hands and everyone fell quiet. "You're right, they're not."

The men cheered.

"Just remember," continued Morgan, "we can make all the defiant speeches we want; shake our fists in the air; but after that we're going to have to stand at the barricades and keep them out."

"Then let's do it," shouted Kelly Pike, and a great cheer filled the air.

Tom Mitchell walked up onto the porch beside Morgan. "Settle down," he shouted. "Let me speak!" The men quieted. "Morgan is telling the truth. This turns into a bloody battle, we have to be prepared to make the sacrifice! You prepared to bleed and starve?"

A flood of 'yeses' rose boldly from the crowd.

"And what about your women and children?" asked Mitchell.

There was only silence. Mitchell nodded. "I asked myself that question this morning," he said. "We may have trapped ourselves in a snare of our own making. But as the Bible says, 'Once you put your hand to the plow, there is no use looking back'."

Dan Ketchum stepped forward, looking to Morgan for reassurance. "If we start running low on food, we can hunt. We're all hunters here. There's plenty of deer and grouse and pheasant, and…"

"Not enough to feed everybody," said Morgan. "And how far do you have to travel so the strikebreakers don't here you shoot, and come looking for you?"

"The company store," said Ketchum anxiously. "There's lots of canned goods there."

"For six weeks, maybe," replied Morgan. "Then what?"

Booth McAlister drove up to the rear of the crowd in his truck, and got out. A narrow pathway opened and he walked towards the community hall. He could feel the hard, distrustful eyes staring at him, but he showed no fear. He came up the steps to Morgan.

"I'd like to speak to these men," said Booth. Morgan nodded.

"You men know no good can come from all this," began Booth.

He was answered with a wall of "boos", and shouts for him to go home.

"Here me out," Booth shouted. "Addison Chase telephoned me only minutes ago, saying he wants you men to go back to work before…"

"And people in Hell want ice water," shouted a derisive voice.

The men all laughed.

"You've seen what's out there," said Booth, pointing towards the strikebreakers camp. "They're not here to work the mine!"

No one made a reply; they all knew what he meant.

"Deets and his deputies have blocked all the roads into this area," Booth went on. "Judge Gits has issued an injunction declaring this strike illegal."

"Let's see him serve it," shouted a miner.

"Yeah," added a chorus of hostile voices.

Morgan waited for them to quiet, then: "Addison Chase is never going to negotiate. But if we go back to work, that police force out there will be withdrawn."

"Police force?" yelled Kelly Pike. "They're mercenary bastards!"

The miners agreed loudly.

"Call them what you want," Booth yelled. "They're not going to go away."

"Then we'll damn well send them away," Pike yelled back.

"At the point of a gun?" asked Booth.

"If we have to."

"And a few sticks of dynamite," shouted a miner.

The other miners gave their approval.

"Anything happens to the mine," continued Booth, "you men will go to jail for a long time."

The crowd began to boo and threaten Booth, but he went on.

"What will happen to your families then? How will they survive?"

"They couldn't be any worse off than they are now," shouted a man.

"Don't be so sure," replied Booth.

The threats from the miners grew stronger, and Morgan stepped up beside his brother, and held up a hand. The men grew silent.

"My brother came here to help us," said Morgan, "not threaten us. What's happening here isn't his doing, it's ours."

"But we can't go back to work," said Ketchum.

"That's right, Dan," said Morgan.

"And we can't leave either, can we?" said Ketchum, troubled.

"No," replied Morgan.

"We leave," said Mitchell, "you all know what becomes of us,"

"Bums and vagrants, that's what," shouted Kelly Pike. "Traveling the roads with no food, no money, no place to go."

"And no future for our families," said Morgan.

"Better to die fighting for what we believe in," yelled a man, "than to let Chase win out."

There was no response from the crowd. Reality had suddenly and silently seeped in like a cold, numbing fog.

"I never wanted anything like this to happen," said Morgan. "Never. But no matter how bad the struggle, we've got to go on. We've got to finish this."

"Down with Chase, and down with Harwick," cried an anguished voice.

The miners roared their approval.

The sweat poured down Morgan's pale face as he shouted: "Get your guns!"

The men scattered quickly, heading for their homes; they were a wild mob now.

Booth watched, then turned to Morgan, saying, "Chase has had Gits swear out warrants for you, Mitchell, Ketchum, and Pike."

"Won't be the first time I've been arrested," said Pike, walking up, a wide grin on his face.

Ketchem shook his head. "My wife's going to raise holy hell if I'm thrown in jail."

Mitchell smiled, and gave Ketchum a friendly pat on the back. "Look on the bright side, Dan. It's flattering to have Chase think we're so important."

"I know you meant well, Booth," said Morgan, "but it's all in God's hands now."

Booth gave no reply and walked towards his truck as two young boys came racing past him, and up to Tom Mitchell.

"Pa," said one boy, breathlessly, "we seen 'em."

"Seen 'em up close," said the second boy.

"Seen who?" asked Mitchell.

"The men that come."

"You went out there?" said Mitchell angrily.

"Yeah," answered the boys, smiling and proud.

Mitchell jerked his cap from his head and began slapping the boys about the head and shoulders. They began backing away, their arms protecting their faces.

"Hold on, Tom," said Morgan. "They were only trying to help." He knelt down and motioned for the boys to come to him. He put a hand on each of them and smiled, and they smiled back. "Don't you wild Indians ever do that again, understand? Or I'll whip you myself."

"Yes, sir," they replied shyly.

"Now what did you see?"

"Lots of tents, cases of food. Lots food," said the first boy.

"And lots of guns," said the second boy. "And bullets. Boxes of 'em spillin' all over the ground."

"How many men?" asked Morgan.

The boys grew embarrassed.

"Well," said the first one, "me and Luke don't count so good yet."

"Take a guess," said Morgan.

The boy shrugged as the second boy answered. "There's a lot more of them than there is of us, for sure."

"You did good," said Morgan. "Go on home now."

The boys ran off, grinning.

"And stay there or I'll whip holy hell out of you," Mitchell growled.

Morgan walked to the far corner of the community hall and stared in the direction of the strikebreakers camp.

"More of them than there is of us," said Ketchum, half to himself.

"Got plenty of ammunition, sounds like," said Pike.

"Kelly," said Morgan without turning to him, "check the company store. Bring back all the boxes of cartridges that are there."

Pike turned and ran.

"And Kelly," called Morgan, stopping him. "Leave Zweig a receipt for every box."

"Right," said Kelly and ran on.

"There won't be much ammunition this time of year," said Mitchell. "Zweig only stocks up during hunting season."

"What happens now?" asked Ketchum, looking in the direction of the strikebreakers camp.

"What do you think happens when you drop a lighted match into a bucket of gasoline?" said Mitchell.

———————

As evening came on, the sun flamed red and finally disappeared from a sky of muddy purple, and the darker it got the more campfires could be seen in the Breakers sprawling camp. The night grew unusually quiet. Here and there smaller fires began to move, weaving around in the blackness; moving towards mine seven. There were just enough torches to light the way for the march of the armed men.

The bell in the cupola of the community hall at mine seven began ringing frantically. Armed miners charged out of the houses as the women turned out the lights, and made the children lie down on the floor.

Morgan McAlister and Tom Mitchell, each with a bolt-action rifle, came rushing to the barricade of a line of small coal wagons that had been tipped onto their sides to block the main road into the housing area. There were already two miners on guard there, and one of them was pointing to the distant torches.

"Can't really tell," said the man, "but it looks like a lot of them are comin'."

Morgan turned to his left and watched a hundred miners spread out in a long thin line behind trees and in low depressions in the ground. Stacks of milled timbers, that had been destined for shoring beams deep in the mine shafts and tunnels were piled in haphazard walls. Armed men stood behind them, waiting. To Morgan's right he saw another hundred men disperse among protective barriers of fat wooden barrels, and rusted-out shells of old cars and trucks that had been placed end to end.

"We're sure spread awful thin," said Morgan quietly.

"You want me to bring Pike and his bunch down here?" asked Mitchell.

"No. Leave them up at the mine. The Breakers might try and get around behind us," answered Morgan.

The miners' flicked the safety catches of their rifles to "off", and watched the advance of the torches. The leafy trees and the waist-high scrub brush began to interfere with their view. They heard a loud voice roar out an order, and the torches stopped advancing.

A husky, tall figure came up the main road towards the barricade of overturned coal wagons, stopped, and remained a safe distance away.

"You there," called Garlow loudly, "behind the barricade. Can you hear me?"

"I hear you," Morgan called back.

"We've been deputized to move you people out. One way or another you're going."

"But we like it here," said Morgan.

"Are you McAlister?"

"That's right."

"I got a warrant here for your arrest."

"Bring it over, let's see it."

Garlow laughed. "Take my word for it, it has your name on it."

"And I've got your name," said Morgan.

"Really."

"On a bullet."

Garlow burst out laughing. "That's a good one. Not afraid to die, huh?"

"What about you?"

Garlow began walking backwards down the road, his rifle at the ready. He raised his left hand, and one by one, the torches were lowered and ground out in the dirt.

Morgan and the other miners could only see a dense black wall before them now. Every man's finger lightly touched the trigger of his rifle. Neither the miners or the Breakers made a sound. Then there was the hoot of an owl, but no one was certain if it was an owl or a human. A few minutes passed and the darkness began to fade. The thick mountainous clouds, obscuring the moon, began to part. The crouching silhouettes of the Breakers could be seen moving forward in long ragged rows. They cautiously approached the knee-deep drainage ditches a hundred yards out from the housing area. The loud crack of a rifle shot broke the tense silence and seemed to echo from all directions. The night exploded with volley after volley of gunfire, and the muzzle flashes of hundreds of guns illuminated the shooters and their positions.

Shouting and cursing could be heard from both sides; then the cries of wounded men.

The miners' houses were hit by a rain of stray bullets. Windows were shattered, and the flimsy board siding began to splinter. Children began screaming and crying, and the women did everything they could to comfort and protect them.

The frantic gunfire became one continuous roar, the muzzle flashes lighting the grim, desperate faces of the men behind the guns. Bullets were ricocheting by the hundreds, tearing into the earth, trees, and make-shift barricades. The miners' unprotected cars and trucks parked in front, and beside the houses, rattled under the snapping bullets— windshields shattered and tires popped and went flat, and the cloth roofs were shredded.

A tremendous explosion occurred at the west end of the miners' firing line, and another explosion came at the east end. There was no mistaking the sound of dynamite as it was flung in the direction of the charging Breakers. More sticks of dynamite kept going off and the Breakers began to retreat into the protection of the dark, but kept up a steady fire.

The explosions in front of the west end of the miners' line ceased, then the explosions at the east end stopped also. But the rifle fire was still heavy from both sides. Finally the muzzle flashes on the Breakers side petered out, and then abruptly stopped. The miners continued shooting until Morgan shouted 'cease fire'. The command was relayed along the line of men, but it was almost a full minute before the guns went silent. The night was now filled with the moaning and crying of the wounded and dying.

Morgan peered cautiously over the barricade then stood up. "You all right, Tom?" he asked softly, without turning.

Mitchell stood up, sweat pouring from his face. "Just barely I thought we were done for. Who was throwing the dynamite?"

"Don't know," replied Morgan. "But they deserve a medal."

A miner came running up, panting hard. "Morgan...got six wounded our end of the line...and one dead."

"Who?" asked Morgan.

"Dan Ketchum."

"Christ," said Mitchell.

"Poor Danny," said Morgan.

"He was the one throwing the dynamite at our end of the line," said the man. "When he threw the last one he got it in the head. It was his and Fitzpatrick's idea.

A second miner came running up from the opposite direction of the line, and stopped in front of Morgan.

"One dead, four wounded," reported the man, his chest heaving. "Fitzpatrick took it in the chest. The crazy mick stood up to throw his last stick and they got him."

Morgan turned away and stared in the direction of the Breakers camp. He didn't want anyone to see how affected he was by the deaths. He felt weak and sick, and guilty.

"Think they'll come back again, tonight?" Mitchell asked.

Morgan swallowed hard, saying, "Maybe. We're all going to have to stay right where we are."

"Done," said Mitchell, and looked to the two men beside him. "Pass the word, everyone holds their position."

The two men ran off.

"What about the wounded?" asked Mitchell.

Morgan turned, and Mitchell could see he was shaken. "Take them to their homes," said Morgan. "See if anything can be done for them."

"We gave as good as we got," said Mitchell encouragingly. "That's what counts. Don't let it get to you."

Morgan gave a quick nod. "See to the wounded, Tom."

———

Katherine McAlister stood on the wooden sidewalk outside her house, a shawl pulled tight around her shoulders. She kept looking up and down the street, watching the wounded being carried to their homes, some of the men still moaning, the rest gritting their teeth in agony. The frantic voices of women could be heard in the distance along with the whimpering of frightened children. All the houses remained dark inside.

"Have you seen, Morgan?" Katherine asked anxiously as a miner hurried by.

"Sorry, no," replied the man.

Then Katherine saw Morgan coming up the street, rifle in hand. She gave a soft sigh and calmed herself. "I heard about Dan and Fitzpatrick," she said as Morgan reached her.

"And ten wounded," said Morgan, not looking at her, and went into the house.

He tossed his rifle on the kitchen table where a small candle burned. He turned on the sink tap and began washing his face and hands with cold water.

Katherine came in and sat at the table. She watched Morgan for a moment. "I've some coffee and biscuits ready if…"

"No," said Morgan, leaning his head under the thick stream of water. He grabbed a thin flour sack hanging on a hook next to the sink. He began wiping his head and face then stood staring at the stream of water gushing into the sink.

"We all knew this might happen," began Katherine. "You can't protect all of us."

Morgan began washing his hands again. "Two dead, ten wounded," he said mechanically. "And there'll be more."

"No one's going to blame you."

Morgan shut off the tap and began drying his hands as he came to the table and sat across from Katherine. "I just don't want this all to be for nothing," he said. "These people can't die for nothing." He closed his eyes and the water in his hair dripped onto his face and it looked as if he were crying.

Katherine reached over, put her hand on his. "It won't be for nothing. No one's death here will be. In the end we will make a difference; we will change things. I'm sure of it. God never allows things that happen to us to be for nothing."

Morgan opened his eyes, and in the candle light, Katherine's face seemed golden and proud, and shining. He smiled, and his fear and apprehension began to recede.

The following morning, the streets of Palmyra were noisy with the day's activities, and a hundred rumors concerning the gun battle at mine seven.

Addison Chase sat on the edge of his chair at his desk. His posture was tense, his expression one of boredom. He slowly rubbed the fingers of one hand back and forth across his forehead; his other hand held the telephone receiver to his ear. "Yes, Brewster, yes," he said tiredly.

Judge Gits, seated in a chair near one of the open windows, puffed thoughtfully on a cigar, his hat and walking stick resting on the window ledge. He flicked some cigar ash out the window then studied Addison closely. He could hear the loud, staccato voice coming from the telephone, but couldn't make out what was being said. He raised and eyebrow as Addison glanced over at him and shook his head in disgust.

"You're absolutely right, Brewster," said Addison, placatingly. "As I told you last night I've taken care of everything."

Brewster's growling voice gave a clipped reply and the telephone clicked loudly at his end. With a groan, Addison replaced the telephone receiver in its cradle.

"Is he going back to Chicago soon?" asked Gits.

"Unfortunately, no."

"If he'd have stayed out of this it wouldn't be such a mess," said Gits.

Addison motioned to the telephone. "Call him and tell him."

"I'd rather talk to a concrete water trough. Where the hell is Deets, he's supposed to be here?"

"Probably stumbling over his own feet somewhere," replied Addison.

"You think he's going to be able to keep these strikebreakers in line?" asked Gits with a frown.

"The only thing Deets is good for is arresting drunks."

There was a knock on the office door and the clerk, Jeffers, stuck his head in. "Sheriff Deets is here, sir."

"In with him," said Addison, leaning back in his chair.

Jeffers opened the door wide and Deets rushed in, hat in hand.

"Morning Mr. Chase, morning Judge," said Deets, forcing a smile.

"Have a chair, Curtis," said Addison in a friendly tone.

"I don't have any more news about the fight at the mine," said Deets, sitting quickly. "But I'm going back out there and..."

"That's not why I sent for you," said Addison.

"You still don't know the casualties on the miners' side of this?" asked Gits, puffing on his cigar.

"No. Just the Breakers, judge," answered Deets. "Ten dead, twenty wounded."

"The miners have two dead and ten wounded," said Addison to Gits.

Deets stared at Addison in surprise.

"You sure?" asked Gits.

"Booth McAlister called my home late last night," said Addison, "asking if a doctor could be sent in. I told him no."

"Good for you," said Gits. "Let the bastards bleed."

"Things got bad out there real quick, Mr. Chase," began Deets. "I didn't think…"

"Well, it's going to get worse," said Addison, rubbing his forehead.

"What?" said Deets, his face paling. "How…how can it get worse?"

"Take a guess," said Gits, and gave a grunt of disgust.

Deets kept glancing from Gits to Addison, waiting for his question to be answered.

"Mr. Harwick has decided to bring in more Breakers," said Addison.

"More?" said Deets, his mouth hanging open.

"Three hundred more."

Deets slumped back in his chair. "There'll be an army out there. Who's going to control them?"

"That's your problem," said Gits, tapping his cigar ash out the window.

"I don't have that many deputies," pleaded Deets. "I can't…"

"All I want you and your deputies to do," said Addison, "is make sure all roads in and out of the mine are kept closed; and that Garlow's horde stays where they are. You let Garlow handle the rest of it."

"I already told him to keep his riff-raff out of Palmyra, or they'd be in trouble," said Deets.

"What'd he say to that?" asked Addison.

Embarrassed, Deets glanced at the floor as he said, "He laughed."

"You laugh back?" asked Gits, smiling.

Deets ignored Gits and looked to Addison. "How soon are these other Breakers coming in?"

"Soon," replied Addison. "Garlow has already sent telegrams to his associates in Chicago."

Deets shook his head. "There's going to be an army out there."

"That's what Mr. Harwick wants," said Addison. "You and your deputies had your chance at fixing things."

"But we…"

"No excuses, Curtis," said Addison. "Garlow will handle it now, you just keep an eye on him and his people."

"And keep an eye out for any reporters that show up," added Gits. "Keep them away from the mine, and everybody out there."

"Oh, I am, Judge. My boys just run two off a while ago. And I heard another come in this morning. He's staying at the Palmyra House. I got a man watching."

"Any union agitators around?" asked Addison.

"No, sir. But we're laying for them, don't worry."

"I don't want them in Palmyra, or near the mine."

"We know what to do, Mr. Chase. They won't be here very long we get hold of them."

"And don't make a mess of it, Deets," said Gits.

"No, Judge."

CHAPTER 5

The locomotive came steaming slowly along the tracks near the Breakers' camp. It pushed a long line of boxcars ahead of it as it had the first time. It came to a stop, steam hissing and wheels screeching. Three hundred tired and dirty men began descending from the cars. They looked more like hoboes than a newly sworn-in police force. Their faces were unshaven and haggard, their eyes wide like suspicious dogs. They moved slowly into the camp, scrutinizing the men already there, who looked back with the same untrustful gazes.

Elbowing his way through the rag-tag mob was a tall man with unusually broad shoulders and hands twice the size of a normal person. He had a wide pock-marked face, and half his teeth were missing and the rest had turned black. He could have passed for a freak in a circus sideshow.

"Garlow," the man growled, "where's Garlow?"

"Here!" Grinning broadly, Garlow held out a hand as he walked up. "Bully Boy," he yelled.

The two shook hands roughly, and punched each other hard in the shoulder with their free hand.

"Well, here we are," said Bully Boy. "Bums, thugs, thieves, and cut-throats every one of them."

"Made to order," said Garlow. "You bring plenty of whiskey?"

"All we can swallow," replied Bully Boy. "And something extra," he added, pointing to the last boxcar.

Standing in the open doorway of the car were eighteen females of all shapes, sizes, and descriptions; each dressed in a bright yellow dress and shoes. A bright yellow bow was pinned in their hair, in an attempt to make them look years younger, and a little delicate, but it didn't quite succeed.

Garlow laughed, and slapped Bully Boy hard on the shoulder. "You brought the dumb Dutchman and his all-girl orchestra. I like that."

"Well, I figured we could all do with a good late night concert," grinned Bully Boy.

The two men roared with laughter.

"Otis, Otis," said a small bearded man, dressed in a faded plaid suit and vest. A battered bowler hat was perched on top his bald head. He hurried towards Garlow, holding out a pale, bony hand.

"Hildschiemer," said Garlow, shaking the man's hand. "I thought you'd be hanged by now."

"No, no," replied Hildschiemer in a matter-of-fact tone. "You need witnesses and evidence for dat."

He turned to the girls in the boxcar. A huge mob of men had already gathered; whistling and calling to the women.

"You like mein delicate daffodils?" asked Hildschiemer. "Mein young chickadees?"

"To tell the truth," answered Garlow, "they look more like old hens from here."

"No, no, no," said Hildschiemer, insulted.

"And a couple of them look like old roosters," added Bully Boy.

As Garlow and Bully Boy had a good laugh, Hildschiemer shook his head angrily, very offended.

"Mein ladies are all fine artistes," said Hildschiemer strongly. "Experienced musicians, all."

"Yeah, I'm sure their very experienced," said Garlow. "Just make sure they don't drink up all the whiskey."

"Mein daffodils don't…"

"Get your delicate flowers set up," said Garlow. "There's plenty of extra tents.

"It's always a pleasure doing business with you, Otis."

"There's lots of money to be had here, Dutchman," said Garlow. "Lots of it."

"I sensed this as we came in," replied Hildschiemer. "And the change of scenery will do my ladies fine. Chicago was starting to put such a rough edge on them, I…"

"They ain't armed, are they?" asked Garlow.

"Well," shrugged Hildschiemer, "when you're in Chicago you have to…"

"They cause any trouble, they'll have to deal with me, and they won't like it," said Garlow, poking Hildschiemer in the chest.

"They're not bad musicians," said Bully Boy seriously. "If you keep your fingers in your ears."

Hildschiemer stared up at Bully Boy, his face puckered tightly as if he'd been slapped, but gave no reply, waiting for Bully Boy and Garlow to stop laughing.

"Let's have a concert tonight," said Garlow. "Hear what they sound like."

"Then they can give another concert later, in their tents," added Bully Boy, "and we can hear what that sounds like."

Bully Boy gave Hildshiemer a resounding slap on the back. Feeling insulted, once again, Hildschiemer gave a quick nod and hurried away.

"He's always been sensitive about his sluts," said Bully Boy. "Don't know why."

"Come on," said Garlow, starting to walk, "we've more important things to discuss."

Bully Boy put his arm around Garlow's shoulder, saying, "I almost fell down and foamed at the mouth when your telegram said ten dollars a day per man."

Garlow grinned. "When's the last time you saw them kind of wages?"

"Never."

"You know, this Harwick and Chase, they've got more money than we could spend in a life time," said Garlow.

"I've always liked the way you do things, Otis. It's always profitable."

Garlow stopped and motioned. "That may be a coal mine up there, but there's a gold mine down here."

"How so?"

"The longer this strike goes, the more money to be had. The thing to do is get out our milking stools and see how much milk this old cow's got in her."

"Slow and steady goes the race, hey?" said Bully Boy with a wink.

"Very slow."

As tents, blankets, and guns were issued to the three hundred new arrivals, there were three men who moved off from the main camp. They pitched their tent in an area of dense scrub brush, not wanting to be a part of the others. Their clothes were thread-bare, their caps were limp and sagging around their ears. The leader of the three, known as Gentleman Jim, stood quietly, his shrewd eyes studying the immense camp, not far off, while his two companions tightened the tent ropes.

"When we going to eat?"

Jim turned to the man who had spoken—an ape-like man who was all muscle. His head was odd-shaped, as were his lips, and his round eyes seemed as if they were going to pop from their sockets. His words had been slow and intense.

"One thing at a time, Oracle," said Jim. "Patience, please."

"I'm going to like it here," said Oracle, looking around excitedly. "This is better than being at..."

"Now, now," interrupted Jim, "we all agreed not to mention that any more."

"I was just going to say, 'that place'. It was nice at Christmas time though; with the lighted tree and all the men singing, and...and the big supper they gave us. I just ate and ate and..."

"Yes, but that's in the past now. We've a new life ahead of us."

"A life of opportunity, huh, Jim?" said Oracle, smiling.

"Exactly."

The third man laughed as he pounded a tent peg deeper into the ground with a rock. He was young and lean, his hair thick and curly. He closely resembled the statue of Michelangelo's, David. And was just as handsome—and that was his nickname. His artless smile held a tint of mischief. But his eyes were cold—impersonal.

"I've never seen a more worthless bunch of bindle-stiffs in my life," said Handsome.

"Yes," replied Jim, looking to the main camp again. "They do remind you of a horde of cannibals."

"Idiots on the loose," said Oracle, shaking his fingers at the sea of men.

"Well, we can't expect to meet many pleasant people in our line of work," said Jim.

"At least the money's good," said Handsome, pounding on another tent peg.

"Yes, but my instincts tell me there could be endless opportunity here. We just have to keep our noses to the wind."

"Opportunity for what?" asked Handsome.

Jim shrugged. "Ten dollars a day is wonderful, but the fellas that operate this coal mine are filthy with greenbacks."

"Money is good, huh, Jim?" said Oracle, taking a piece of rock-hard bread from his coat pocket. He snapped off a tiny crumb and began gnawing on it.

Jim smiled. "You're a quick learner, Oracle. Like a sponge soaking up water. Yes, money is good, but not people. They do such horrible things to get hold of those little pieces of green paper. It never ceases to fascinate me how rotten human beings are."

"No," said Oracle, shaking his head, very serious, "people have always been kind to me. Except when we were in…in that place. People are good, I think. Good like money."

"Then let's fill our pockets and get out of here," said Handsome. "The quicker the better."

"I agree," replied Jim. "Life's a lousy deal at best, and I'm tired of drifting with nothing to show for it. Hoboing it, year after year."

"Sometimes I'd like to walk through life on my hands," said Oracle.

"Why?" asked Handsome, chuckling.

"To see the world a different way. Maybe upside down things would be better."

"Yeah, maybe life would be better upside down," said Handsome, dropping to the ground and leaning against a decayed tree stump. "But right now it's a son-of-a-bitch."

"Could be we've drifted into something good this time," said Jim.

"The land of milk and honey," said Oracle, still crunching on his dry crust of bread.

Jim and Handsome laughed, and Oracle joined in, clapping his hands; he loved to laugh.

"If Oracle is correct," said Jim, "and this is the land of milk and honey, I suggest we rake around and see what we can find."

A heavy frown appeared on Oracle's face. "But what about him?"

"Who?" asked Jim.

"The man who brought us here. He has a shadowy soul, Jim."

"A dark soul is more like it," smiled Jim. "Bully Boy will bear watching, but we've always prevailed. As long as we stick together."

"Nothing can hurt us if we do that," said Oracle, sucking on the tiny piece of bread he had left.

———————

At the east of the Breakers' camp, where the main road angled in a wide circle towards mine seven's housing area, two large dump trucks blocked the entire roadway. Nearby, two armed deputies lounged in the shade of a tree, smoking thinly rolled cigarettes, their pump shotguns across their laps. Their hats were pulled low, and they seemed half asleep in the cool breeze that drifted over them. When the distant sound of an automobile engine reached their ears they threw their cigarettes down and got quickly to their feet.

A small Chevy roadster came up the dusty road, its narrow tires hardly had any tread on them, and the black body of the automobile was dull from age and neglect. One of the deputies moved to the middle of the road, holding his hand up. The other deputy stood with his shotgun at the ready.

"Morning, gentlemen, morning," said the driver cheerfully, a wide grin on his suntanned face.

The deputies eyed him suspiciously. The man was dressed simply and cleanly. A straw hat sat cocked to one side of his head, and his bright red bow tie stood out boldly against his smooth white shirt and thin summer suit. He had the look of a confident business man.

"If you're another one of them reporters," said the first deputy, "turn this junk heap around and head for the county line."

"And don't look back," said the second deputy.

"Easy, fellas, easy," said the man, the broad smile never leaving his face. "Relax those hackles." He took a small business card from the wide satin band of his straw hat and handed it to the nearest deputy.

"Roscoe Brodie's the name," he said proudly. "Traveling salesman extraordinaire, and a friend to man, I like to think."

"Selling what?" asked the second deputy, approaching the auto on the passenger side, his finger still on the trigger of his shotgun.

"Insurance, sir," replied Brodie cheerfully. "The saviour of the working stiff."

"What kind of insurance?" asked the first deputy, tossing the business card to the ground.

"Miners' insurance. The best insurance..."

The deputies began laughing and lowered their shotguns. Brodie waited patiently as the two men kept laughing and staring at him as if he were a lunatic.

"You sure come down the wrong road, insurance man," said the second deputy.

"You know what's going on here?" asked the other deputy.

Brodie's face grew serious as he glanced back and forth at the two men. "Why no," he said. "I just arrived in the area, and..."

"There's a mad-dog strike on here, and you don't want to get in the middle of it," said the second deputy.

"Strike?" said Brodie, shocked. "If I'd a known that, I'd a never come near the place."

"Well, you ain't going to sell any insurance here," said the first deputy, "so just back on..."

"Now wait a minute," said Brodie, holding up his hands. "Wait just a heartbeat. This stumbling block could be a stepping stone."

The deputies looked at each other, confused.

"If there's a dangerous strike going on," continued Brodie, "what better chance of selling life insurance?"

The first deputy burst out laughing, but the other deputy leaned on the auto door, eyeing Brodie hard.

"Somebody must have hit you on the head with a brick," said the deputy.

"Think about it," replied Brodie, undeterred. "These people could be scared enough to let loose of some money if they think I got a policy to protect life and limb. Part of such a policy is to cover strikes just like…"

"When we're done with those poor bastards up there," said the first deputy, "they won't have a pot to piss in, let alone money to buy one."

"I disagree, I disagree," said Brodie, and opened a small battered suitcase beside him on the front seat. He took out a pint bottle of whiskey and handed it to the first deputy, then handed a second pint to the other deputy. "Virgins," said Brodie.

"Huh?" said the two men.

"Never been opened."

The two deputies broke the seals, pulled out the corks, and took a long swallow.

"Tell you what I'd like to do," said Brodie. "Let me go on up there, talk to some of them people. I won't stay long, promise. Just want to see if there's any business to be had. If not I'll hurry right back."

"You're nutty as a wooden watch," said the first deputy, taking another swallow from his bottle.

"You fellas ain't got nothing to lose," said Brodie, smiling. "Matter of fact, when I come back out, I might be able to hunt up another couple pints of that stuff. Good, ain't it?"

The two men looked at one another then Brodie.

"I don't know," said the first deputy. "Something like this could get us in trouble."

"How's this," said Brodie, leaning close to the deputy. "While I'm in there, I can get look around, listen to what's going on. Find out what those folks are up to. Could put you fellas in real good with the sheriff."

The deputy thought a moment then nodded. "All right, but don't take all day about it."

"You won't regret this, I guarantee it," said Brodie, rubbing his hands together. "This is your lucky day."

"Yeah, yeah," said the second deputy. "Go on, get the hell out of here."

The first deputy climbed into the cab of one of the dump trucks, started it up, and backed out of the way. The gears of Brodie's roadster grated together, and he waved cheerfully as he drove away towards the mine.

The deputy started to drive the dump truck back onto the road when he heard a horn sound three long blasts. Coming up the road was a caravan of ten double-wheeled, flatbed trucks, each carrying a three thousand gallon water tank strapped securely behind the cab.

The second deputy began motioning to the right as the trucks got nearer. They turned off the road in the direction of the Breakers' camp.

When the men in camp saw the approaching trucks a tremendous shout went up, and group after group began grabbing buckets, and pots, and pans in preparation for their daily ration of water.

Three crude outdoor kitchens had been set up where a gang of sweaty, cursing, spitting cooks prepared all the meals; and each morning, before sunrise, a short train of six boxcars steamed in loaded with sacks of flour and beans, canned corned beef, and barrels of salt pork, then chugged away to Palmyra to load up again for the next day.

Sheriff Deets roamed tensely through the chaos of men and dust, smoking campfires and steaming pails of coffee. Every so often he'd stop, and his eyes would search in all directions. Four deputies were behind him, their shotguns cradled in their arms.

Deets grabbed the collar of a hunch-backed, wild-eyed man dressed in a long ragged coat and slouch hat, and wearing no shoes. The man put up an arm, thinking he was going to be hit.

"Where's Garlow?" asked Deets.

"Garlow? Garlow?" said the man, thinking hard. "Don't know no Garlow, no." He broke away and scurried off towards the water trucks, waving a rusty tin cup. "Nobody named Garlow here."

"Wonder what asylum they pulled him out of," said Deets.

"There he is," said one of the deputies, pointing.

Garlow stood stripped to the waist in front of a large tent as another man doused water on his head and neck from a wooden bucket. Garlow roughly rubbed the water over his face, neck, chest, and protruding belly, moaning all the time from the pleasure of the coolness.

"More," said Garlow, rubbing harder, and the man tipped the bucket again.

"Garlow," said Deets, walking up, "what the hell's going on?"

Garlow turned to Deets and shook his thick hair and beard, spraying water into the air like a dog shaking itself dry. Deets stepped back quickly, his hand moving to the revolver on his hip.

"Don't it ever cool down in this hell-hole of a wilderness?" asked Garlow.

Deets just glared and said nothing.

Garlow smiled and held out a dripping hand. "Nice to see you again, law dog."

Deets kept his hand near his gun.

"Did I hear you say, 'what the hell's going on'?"

"You were hired to get those miners out. So far you've just been lying around eating and collecting wages."

"I have to assume you weren't here a few nights ago," said Garlow. "When we went over there, and the miners started throwing sticks of dynamite like it was confetti. So now we have to rest up; renew our strength."

"Fine," said Deets, unsympathetically, "but when you going back over there?"

Garlow looked Deets up and down. "Got a lot of hard bark on you, don't you law dog?"

"Mr. Chase and Mr. Harwick are becoming unhappy over this delay," said Deets. "They want their money's worth, and soon. They're making me unhappy, so I'm here to make you unhappy."

Garlow laughed, slapped his hands together, and bent his head down. "Water!"

The man beside him emptied the bucket onto Garlow's neck. Deets waited, but Garlow simply kept washing his hair and face, and sighing.

"More," yelled Garlow.

"I'll get some," said the man with the bucket, and ran off.

"Here, have mine," said a voice.

Garlow looked up. Handsome stood there with a full bucket of water dangling from one hand.

"Thank you, son," said Garlow, and bent forward.

Handsome began pouring water on him.

"I want to know when you're going to get back to business," said Deets, motioning towards the mine.

Garlow raised his head and shook his wet hair and beard. Deets clutched the handle of his revolver, almost drawing it.

"This isn't as easy as you people think," replied Garlow, rubbing his hairy chest and belly.

"It's dangerous," said Handsome, looking Deets up and down.

"The boy's right," said Garlow. "Very dangerous. We have to plan carefully."

"And how long's this planning of yours going to take?"

Garlow shrugged. "We have to consider things. Unexpected things. Dangerous things."

"What the hell's that mean?" asked Deets, frustrated.

Garlow's eyes and face grew grim and sinister looking. "When I'm ready to move on the mine, we'll move. And then you can take care of all the bodies. Until then, don't worry about what me and my men are doing."

"Mr. Harwick says you're wasting time, and he…" Deets stopped when he heard the screeching of violins and cellos, and the blaring of tinny trombones.

Looking in the direction of a sparse grove of tall, scraggily maple trees, far across the camp, Deets could just make out the all-girl orchestra in their bright yellow dresses. They were seated on rickety wooden folding chairs, with rusty, wobbly music stands in front of them. Hildschiemer stood on an overturned washtub, holding a short stick in his hand. He was waving it back and forth, trying to stay in time with the music.

"What the hell is this?" asked Deets, taking a few steps forward.

"They're practicing for the concert tonight," replied Garlow. "Man does not live by bread alone."

"What the hell's that tune they're playing?" said Deets, puzzled.

"In the Good Old Summer Time," answered Garlow. "It's all the rage in Chicago."

"It doesn't sound like anything," said Deets.

"You're obviously not a music lover," replied Garlow.

Deets pointed to him. "Mr. Harwick and Mr. Chase want this strike settled. So if you want to keep getting paid, do your job or get out."

"We'll get out when we're ready to," said Garlow, and leaned his head down.

Handsome began pouring water on Garlow's neck from his bucket.

Deets started to say something then turned and stalked off, followed by his deputies.

———————

Gentleman Jim stood a little ways from where he, Oracle, and Handsome had pitched their tent. He was studying the huge dirty buildings of mine seven. His gaze then turned to the battered houses of the miners.

Oracle sat cross-legged on the ground, gorging on spoonfuls of red beans and greasy chunks of corned beef. A biscuit, the size of his fist, set in the middle of the oily mess. Oracle sighed contentedly with each mouthful he took.

"Jim," he said, his cheeks puffed out with food. "Eat. This is good."

"I'm doing fine, thank you," replied Jim, without turning. He dipped a broken piece of biscuit into a tin cup filled with coffee. As he chewed, he glanced at the biscuit then tossed it away. "I'm afraid the cuisine here leaves a lot to be desired." He gestured to his untouched plate of beans and corned beef setting beside Oracle. "Be my guest."

Oracle snatched the plate, dumped it onto his, and continued eating.

Handsome walked up quietly, carrying a full bucket of water, and dropped it near Oracle.

Jim turned to him, asking, "Any news?"

"Some," said Handsome.

"Get some food, Handsome," said Oracle. "You need to eat." He dipped his tin cup into the bucket and scooped out some water.

"There's gallons of coffee over there,' said Handsome. "Go get it."

"No," said Oracle, shaking his head. "Water. Water is life."

Handsome grinned and so did Jim.

"Speaking of life," began Jim, "we need to get ours moving. What have you heard?"

"Interesting things," replied Handsome, squatting beside the water bucket. He dipped his hands in then wiped his face.

"Interesting, how?" asked Jim, taking a sip of his coffee.

"These gutless bindle-stiffs are here on vacation. They're all talk and no action."

"Tell me more," said Jim, kneeling down.

"Garlow's stalling."

"Yes," agreed Jim, "he's knows easy money when he smells it."

"But the sap that's paying the bills isn't happy."

"Harwick Coal Company," said Jim, nodding.

"Rumor has it, this Harwick doesn't live far from here."

"Anything else?"

"Harwick, and a fella named Chase, want something done now. Want the miners out, now."

Jim looked towards the mine. "Maybe we'll find a diamond in the mud yet."

"How so?" asked Handsome.

Jim stood up, walked a few paces away, and stood staring at the distant houses. Handsome came up behind him.

"I need you to do me a favor, Handsome."

"Sure."

"Tonight, when it's good and dark, over there, have a look around. Listen carefully to what you hear. Then come back and tell me what you know."

Handsome smiled. "Easy as pie."

"But be discreet," said Jim, holding up a finger for emphasis. "I need you back here with me."

"I won't have any trouble," said Handsome, and took a long folded knife from his coat pocket. With a flick of his wrist, a six inch blade snapped open, shiny and razor sharp.

"I'm still hungry," said Oracle.

Jim and Handsome watched Oracle lick his tin plate clean.

"I sometimes wonder if he's human or animal," said Handsome softly.

"Yes," replied Jim with a tender smile, "I feel more like his keeper than a friend. But he's useful."

CHAPTER 6

Even with the rising wind, the night air was muggy and had a heaviness to it. The darkenss concealed most of the mine buildings and houses of mine seven. No lights were permitted for fear the Breakers would come in close to spy, or mount another attack. Guards roamed the entire area, but not nearly as many men as the night before. They were spread out dangerously thin.

At the far end of the housing area, the community hall had become filled with armed miners. Candleholders had been nailed along the walls, and stubs of candles placed in them and lighted, providing a meager glow. All the windows and doors stood open, and outside, clusters of women stood looking in, some with babies in their arms. The soft light of the flickering candles barely illuminated the huge room. The miners talked quietly among themselves; some passed small sacks of tobacco and cigarette papers around; some miners passed pint bottles of whiskey.

Morgan McAlister, Tom Mitchell, and Kelly Pike stood at the rear of the humid room, facing the miners. Finally Morgan took a step forward.

"Men," he said loudly, "your attention, please."

Roscoe Brodie moved out of the shadows from behind Mitchell and Pike, and stepped up onto a shaky wooden chair. He stared out at the inquiring faces before him. His straw hat was gone, and his bow tie and coat. The sleeves of his white shirt were rolled up above his elbows and his sharp eyes seemed bright in the faint light. He didn't appear to be the same man who had driven through the road block earlier that morning.

"Sinners," he said loudly. "You're all sinners!" His voice was hard and grim. "It's a sin to give up hope; a sin to lose your courage. Don't be sinners, be heroes! Heroes of your own life. I came here to help you men live like human beings, not animals. The American Miners' Association is going to help you win what you've started. There's no turning back! It's win or die! But you can't do it alone. This one mine can't survive alone. You may think you can, but you're wrong."

"And your union is here to save us all from holy hell, that it?" shouted a miner.

"Yes," shouted Brodie. "If we unite!"

"We've had lots of you union boys come through here over the years," said an angry voice from the back of the room. "You promise this and that, but when the mine owners, and the law, get tough, you talkers fade away like ghosts."

The entire room voiced their agreement.

"Not this time," replied Brodie. "We're prepared for battle, just like you. And we got money. Money, not bullets. Money just like these scavenging coal barons who bluff you into thinking they're God Almighty!"

"They are God Almighty," yelled a miner.

"Only if you believe they are," said Brodie, and jumped down from his chair. He began moving through the crowd, looking into the faces of the men near him. When he came to a man who was horribly scarred—skin wrinkled like old newspaper—he stopped. There was true compassion in Brodie's eyes, but the scarred man looked down, embarrassed.

"Mine fire?" asked Brodie.

The man nodded in answer.

Brodie walked on, and the men gave way before him. He saw a man with a crudely carved peg-leg, where his right leg should have been.

"Where's your leg?" asked Brodie.

"Still in shaft four, with twelve dead friends," replied the man, flippantly. "The whole damn thing caved in."

Brodie moved on. He spied a stoop-shouldered man, holding his deformed hands at his waist; hands that looked like lobster claws.

"Still working in the shafts?" said Brodie.

The man gave a smirk. "What do you think?"

"Then how come you're still here?"

"I collect the garbage, and the coal ashes from the cook stoves of all the houses," replied the man.

"And you're allowed to live in one of those run-down shacks out there?" said Brodie with a touch of bitterness.

"That," replied the man, "and a dollar a day wages."

"Your masters are very kind, aren't they?"

The man looked down, not wanting to answer.

"And when you're no longer able to haul garbage and coal ashes," said Brodie, "what will happen to you?"

The man continued staring down, saying nothing. Everyone knew what would happen.

"You get crippled and maimed, working in unsafe mines," said Brodie, looking around, "but it's not the owners fault, is it? No. They blame you! It's always you're fault! I came through that road block, today, by giving a spiel about selling miners' insurance. They laughed. And they should have. There's no miners insurance worth a damn anywhere. But the mine owners get all the insurance they want for their mines! They spend thousands and thousands of dollars every year. But what about you? You get hurt, and you either have to get well or die, or be thrown on the scrap heap along with the ashes from your coal stoves!"

Brodie approached the wide, open doors at the opposite end of the hall, his sympathetic gaze still on the men around him. From a dark corner, near the doors, the smooth, tanned face of Handsome appeared briefly in the glow of a candle, then receded. But his cold-eyed stare remained on Brodie.

"Can you read?" Brodie asked a man. "Can you read?" he asked another.

The two men shook their heads.

"Why not?" Brodie said angrily.

"Well," said one of the men, sheepishly, "we...we don't have the time. We have to work. Always working."

Brodie stopped before a tall, gaunt miner whose face was drawn and criss-crossed with deep dark lines.

"How old are you?" asked Brodie.

"Thirty, sir."

"You look a hundred."

The man smiled weakly. "I feel like a hundred."

"You go down the shafts everyday, not knowing if you'll come back up alive, don't you?"

The man nodded.

"And if the mine don't kill you," continued Brodie, "how soon will the coal dust?"

The man shrugged. "If the black lung starts, I think I'll just crawl into a closet and put a gun barrel in my mouth, and pull the trigger. It'd be easier than the black lung."

Brodie patted the man on the shoulder and walked on. "Pain," he shouted. "Why should any of you have to earn his bread in pain? Are you beasts that walk on two legs, or are you men? You like working in Hell? Dying like rats in the dark? Harwick and Chase have about as much concern for you as they do the pick and shovel you work with. I've seen the mine you slave in; seen your so-called houses. And I've smelled the stink of poverty and oppression!"

"We produce the goods," shouted a miner, no longer able to contain himself, "but Chase and Harwick are the only ones who profit!"

The room exploded in angry voices.

"They scoop up the gravy with one hand," shouted Kelly Pike, "and the cream with the other!"

Every man in the room roared their agreement; and the women, at the windows and doors, joined in.

"Yes, yes, yes," Brodie kept yelling over and over, hurrying back towards the chair he had stood on. "A greedy octopus with slimy tentacles. And they're around your necks, and the necks of your women and children!"

In frustration, the miners began pounding the butts of their rifles against the floor, and the sound became louder and louder—like thunder. Brodie stepped up onto his chair again. There was a trace of a smile on his face; he knew he had them on his side now. He held up his hands.

"Listen to me," he yelled.

Finally the pounding faded to silence.

"There's no way to imprison an idea that's got hold of a man," said Brodie gently. "And this idea has got hold of you—it's got hold of me—and none of us knows exactly what will happen in the end. But we can't let fear stop us. There's a lot of miners out there, just like you, lots of women too, who want to see their children grow up strong and healthy and happy. Those children deserve every chance they can get to become something. Something more than underfed work mules with no future!" he shouted. "The working man made this country, and the working man will save it from people like Harwick and Chase. But you can't do it alone! You've got to organize! Those strikebreakers out there may seem like an overwhelming army, but I can bring in ten times the size of that bunch."

"How?" asked Tom Mitchell.

"Just ask me to," replied Brodie. "The American Miners' Association will come in if you ask us."

"How do we know you're not just another bunch of goddamn Red communists?" yelled Kelly Pike.

The crowd agreed loudly with him.

"Because I say we're not," Brodie yelled back. "Give me the say-so, and I'll bring in enough men to surround that Breakers camp. Every newspaper in the state will find out your side of this; not the Harwick Coal Company side of it. We can even petition the governor for help!"

"He doesn't even know we exist," shouted a miner.

"He will before I'm done. The entire country will. We can put pickets clear around the town of Palmyra; make Chase and Harwick holler 'uncle'. What do you say?"

The hall grew quiet, and all eyes went to Morgan McAlister.

"What say you, Morgan?" asked one of the miners near him.

Morgan glanced around at the shadowy, staring faces. "I brought all you men into this," he began, "your women and children, too. I thought this situation of ours could be settled with words, not guns. I was wrong. I'm sorry for that. Friends of ours have died. There can't be any more. I agreed to let Mr. Brodie speak because he's convinced me he can go back out there and accomplish something. Something quick. We can't allow ourselves to be surrounded and killed off one by one, or starved out. If Mr. Brodie can deliver what he says he can, then I say we have to stand with him. I trust his words, and I believe him."

"So do I," said Tom Mitchell.

"When I leave here in the morning," answered Brodie, "and get past those deputies on the road, I only have to send one telegram from Palmyra. From then on your lives will change forever. I give my word. But you have to hold on, you have to endure."

"Mr. Brodie," said Morgan, "we have to win, not just endure."

Brodie got down from his chair and held out his hand to Morgan. "I promise you I'll be back."

"Then do what you have to do," said Morgan, shaking hands, and the hall erupted in cheering.

Pulling his cap down close to his eyes, Handsome didn't look any different from the mob of men making their way out of the hall. Once outside he looked back, studying the faces of Morgan, Brodie, Mitchell, and Pike. As he turned to go another face caught his attention; a girl, just off to the side of the main doors. She was young and tall, and the thin cotton dress she wore flowed around the firm curves of her body like water. Her face was perfect. Handsome smiled, and her crystal blue eyes looked into his, boldly, impishly. Handsome stepped in close to her as the miners continued filing out of the hall.

"You sure have pretty hair," Handsome whispered. "Like hot, shiny tar. Even smells good."

"I just washed it," replied the girl, running her wolfish eyes up and down Handsome's lean body. She tilted her head back, revealing a graceful, pure white neck.

"What's your name?" asked Handsome.

"Naomi."

"Pretty. Like you."

Naomi gave a slight smile. "What's your name?"

"Guess."

"No. Tell me."

"Rumplestiltskin."

Naomi laughed softly. "That's no name." She took a long look at his face now. "I don't remember seeing you around before."

Handsome leaned back against the frame of the doorway, waiting for the crowd to thin out. He winked at Naomi, and took a small sack of tobacco and cigarette papers from his coat pocket. She watched his every move. He gently rolled a cigarette with his slender fingers, then snapped a match to life with his thumbnail. After taking a deep drag, and blowing the smoke out though his nose, he offered the cigarette to Naomi. She made a quick glance around, to make sure no one was watching, took the cigarette and inhaled deeply. She blew the smoke, long and slow, into Handsome's face. He grinned.

"You sure ain't no miner," said Naomi.

"How so?"

"I ain't never seen no coal miner with clean fingernails and smooth hands."

Handsome took the cigarette back and stuck it in the corner of his mouth. "And I ain't never seen a woman as beautiful as you."

"What you doin' here?"

"I come to join the fight. I think what you people are doing is awful right."

"You a friend of Morgan McAlister's?"

"I'm a friend to anybody that stands up against these rich, thieving robber barons."

"Where you stayin'?"

"Where *you* staying?

"Why?"

Handsome winked at her again. "I might just come calling some moonlit night."

"Why?" said Naomi, teasingly.

Handsome smiled and handed her the cigarette. "So I can sit and smell that perfumed hair of yours. Smells like roses. You like roses, I'll bring you some?"

"You ain't got no roses."

"What color you like?"

"Big pink ones," she said, taking a drag on the cigarette and handing it back.

"Ever seen big pink ones?"

"Once. The superintendent's sister grows roses; the mean, old biddy. She never gives any to anybody; just lets them dry up and die."

"Well, I'll bring you lots of pink roses. Where's your house?"

"Maybe I don't want you at my house."

Handsome stepped close and breathed a warm, strong breath on her neck from his nostrils. "I say you do," he whispered.

Naomi took a second or two to decide, then motioned with her thumb. "Down that way, on the right. There's a big, old bulldog chained to a tree. And he don't like sweet-talkin' men."

"He'll whine and slobber when he sees me," replied Handsome with a smile.

"Naomi," called a gruff male voice.

Naomi turned quickly as a surly looking man—broad-shouldered, and a neck as thick as a bull's—came through the thinning crowd.

"Yeah, pa?" she said sourly.

"Who you talkin' to there?"

"Oh, he's just..." Naomi stopped when she turned her head and saw Handsome was gone. Her eyes quickly searched the milling groups of armed men, but saw no sign of him; but she still smiled to herself. "Rumpelstiltskin, huh?" she said quietly. "Bet you can't even spell it."

"Go on home," said Naomi's pa, walking up. "You're supposed to be helpin' your ma, you know she's feelin' poorly."

"I wanted to see what was goin' on," replied Naomi with a pout.

"Who was that fella?"

"Said he come to join the strike. He..."

"Go on home for I slap you," interrupted her pa.

Naomi threw a defiant glance at him, but walked away.

Though Naomi had lost sight of Handsome in the darkness, her pa's eyes had stayed on him from his first look, and he began to follow Handsome.

Moving swiftly along the edges of the dispersing groups of men and women, Handsome ducked down a narrow alley between two darkened houses. A huge black dog rushed up to a battered picket fence, barking and snarling, but a thick rope, tied to a fat stake, kept him from following Handsome.

Staying to the rear of the long line of houses, Handsome suddenly heard footsteps behind him, gaining on him. Instead of looking back, he put his hands in his coat pockets, turned into another alley, squeezed past a battered pickup truck, and found himself on the main street again. When he reached the far end of the street, he continued on, leaving the houses behind, and entering a deserted area of tall brush and weeds, and deep shadows.

"Hey?" said a voice, not far behind him.

Handsome didn't stop—his hands still in his pockets. Hard, strong fingers grab his shoulder and spun him around.

"Can't you hear?" said Naomi's pa.

Handsome smiled. "Sorry. Guess I was day dreaming again."

"You was talkin' to my daughter."

Handsome looked off and squinted, thinking. "Oh, the gal at the meeting. Yeah, I was."

Naomi's pa pulled the left side of his coat back, revealing a revolver in the waist band of his pant. Handsome's face remained expressionless, but his right hand knotted into a fist in his coat pocket.

"I been here a long time, boy. I don't ever remember seeing you before."

"Just come in," said Handsome. "Want to join the fight."

"Who asked you to?"

Handsome just shrugged and smiled, and his right hand slipped unnoticed from his coat pocket. "I talked to one of them fellas at the meeting there. That Morgan fella."

"What's his last name?" asked the man, moving in closer.

Handsome thought a moment. "Well…I'm not real good at names, but I think it was…yeah, McAlister."

"Let's go see him."

"Sure," replied Handsome, taking off his cap and scratching his head. "He'll vouch for me. Let's go."

With a hard snap of his wrist, the six inch blade of Handsome's folded knife sprang open, and before Naomi's pa could touch his revolver, Handsome's cap was over his face and partly in his mouth.

Morgan McAlister entered his dark house, set his rifle beside the door, and walked towards the kitchen. "Katherine?" he called out. The house was quiet, but outside groups of men were talking softly as they went to their assigned guard posts for the night.

On the narrow kitchen table was a short, lighted candle, and lying open beside it a worn leather-bound Bible. Morgan tossed his cap on the table, leaned over and stared at the thin white pages. His eyes saw the words, "Do not fear only believe."

"Is it that simple?" Morgan asked himself. "Just believe?" A little further down the page he saw: 'And they laughed at Him'. Morgan closed the book and shoved it away. There were footsteps on the porch and he turned as the screen door opened and Katherine entered.

"You shouldn't be out running around in the dark," said Morgan. "The Breakers could start shooting."

"Well, these thin walls don't provide much protection against lead bullets," said Katherine, "Besides, it was an emergency."

"Where?"

"Molly O'Donnell and her baby took real sick. I went to see what I could do. And Mrs. Tyrone's three kids aren't getting fed proper, they're losing weight; I took some food over."

"I wonder if the women and children will pay a bigger price than us men," said Morgan, closing his tired eyes.

Katherine's hands rubbed his face gently. "You sure are getting scruffy, you need a shave. I need to see that handsome, smiling face again."

Morgan forced a smile and kissed her hand. "You been reading the Book again.

"It helps me."

"Words. Words from Brodie; words from the Bible. Will it do any good in the end?"

Katherine gave him a playful slap on the face. "Don't blaspheme," she said, and crossed to the other side of the kitchen and opened the small refrigerator. "I fixed a plate for you. You haven't eaten all day."

"I'll get it later," replied Morgan, letting himself down into a chair at the table.

"You've got to eat," said Katherine, putting the plate in front of him. "And you need sleep. I hear you up in the middle of the night, pacing."

"Wish I was a drinking man, then I could get drunk and take away the pain."

"What happened at the meeting?"

"Brodie gave a rousing speech, and we all listened. God help us, I think he's the only hope we got right now."

"He still staying with us tonight?"

"Yes. He wanted to walk around a while; keep talking to everybody; keep making promises."

"Promises he can't keep?"

Morgan shrugged. "I don't know what more there is I can do." He folded his arms on the table and stared into the darkness. His voice was filled with despair. "Are any of us strong enough, clever enough, to make our dreams come true? I have a haunting, unforgiving fear that we can't."

Katherine sat across from Morgan and took his hand. "At times life's a hard game to play. At least for people like us. We can't give up on ourselves, Morgan," she said, and squeezed his hand tighter.

"How much luck does it take?"

"Luck has nothing to do with it, it's…"

Katherine was cut short by heavy boots stomping onto the front porch, then a frantic pounding on the screen door. "Morgan, you in there?" yelled Kelly Pike.

Morgan rushed out of the kitchen, followed by Katherine. Pike opened the screen door and stepped in, his face red and covered with sweat. He clutched his rifle tightly in one hand.

"What's wrong?" asked Morgan.

"They just found Snider, far end of the street in the bushes. His throat's been cut."

"Alert all the men," replied Morgan. "Get them outside. The Breakers could be coming."

Pike plunged out the door. Morgan and Katherine followed, and came to the middle of the main street as Tom Mitchell hurried up. Not far behind him were a group of men; two with lighted lanterns, and four others carrying the body of Snider in a blanket.

"Did Pike tell you?" asked Mitchell.

"Just now," answered Morgan.

"We're taking him home. It's not going to be easy on his wife and kids."

"I'll go there now," said Katherine, and rushed away.

"Can you come too, Morgan?" asked Mitchell.

"Of course, let me…"

Morgan stopped, and he and Mitchell watched the men go by with the body.

"That makes five," said Mitchell quietly.

As the men proceeded up the street, people began coming out of their houses to see what was happening.

"Tom, I need a word with you," said Morgan, and walked back to the porch of his house and sat down.

"What is it?" said Mitchell.

"If you and the others want someone else to head the committee, just…"

"What?" said Mitchell surprised. "You can't mean that."

"I don't want to let you people down. I can't."

"You won't. If we didn't trust you, you wouldn't be leading us now."

"What if you don't trust yourself?" said Morgan, wringing his hands. "What if you lose your courage?"

Mitchell, suddenly looking worn-out and defeated, sat down beside Morgan and spoke softly. "I know. There are times I feel a horrible emptiness coming over me. And I can't sleep, can't eat, can't think straight."

"Yes."

Mitchell lowered his head and stared blindly. "It's worse when you have to give your kids less and less to eat every day; listen to them cry themselves to sleep at night, because their bellies are getting emptier and emptier."

"I'm praying Brodie can do something," said Morgan, "before it's too late."

"From your mouth to God's ear," said Mitchell.

———

Hope McAlister stood at the edge of the porch of the superintendent's house staring down the main street, watching a large crowd gather; some with lighted lanterns. Booth McAlister drove up in front of the house in his truck, the headlights went off and he got out. As he approached the porch, he glanced up the street.

"Something happen?" he asked Hope.

"They just carried somebody by in a blanket," replied Hope.

"Was Morgan with them?"

"Don't know. Maybe it was him in the blanket."

Booth threw a hostile glance at Hope, and went on into the house. Hope followed. When she reached the doorway of the kitchen, Booth's shirt sleeves were rolled up, and he was washing his hands and forearms in the sink.

"You shouldn't have any of these lights on," said Booth. "The Breakers could start shooting."

"Let them, I'm not afraid."

Booth ignored her, and began wiping his hands and arms with a small towel. "You eat yet?" he asked.

"Been waiting for you. You go to that meeting they had earlier?"

"No. I was up at the mine. There was trouble with one of the pumps."

"You should have gone. Found out what..."

"I don't think I would have been all that welcome, do you?" He threw the towel in the sink, crossed to the refrigerator, near the stove, and opened the narrow door.

"You should have gone any way," said Hope.

"Why?" said Booth, taking a small, greasy chicken leg out of a bowl.

"Addison Chase is going to get rid of you, you don't start doing your job."

Booth slammed the refrigerator door shut and turned to Hope. "Well, I don't give a damn what Chase and Harwick think, any more."

"You're taking Morgan's side?"

Booth threw the chicken leg against the wall, and took a step towards Hope. "You want me to lick Chase's boots, that it? Turn my back on these people? I've done enough of that. Maybe you don't care, but now I do."

"You're just like your brother," said Hope angrily. "No backbone!" She hobbled away, her two canes jabbing against the wood floor. "I hate these miners," she shouted. "And this town; and its filth and grime!"

"Then leave," Booth shouted back.

Hope stopped and looked back over her shoulder. There was only bitterness and hate in her eyes.

Booth gave a helpless gesture with his hands. "Hope, I didn't…"

Once outside, Hope moved to the far end of the front porch, and sat in a sagging wicker chair. There were tears streaming down her cheeks. Booth came quietly out the screen door, and went and sat on the porch railing.

"You're not going to change what's already happened," he said. "Or what's going to happen."

"I hate this place; this rotten life; my rotten legs."

"And your rotten brothers?"

Hope started to say something, then her hands went quickly to her legs, and she began rubbing them hard.

"You need your pills?" asked Booth concerned.

"No. I already took them. They don't do any good any way. It's always worse at night for some reason."

"You should see a doctor again. See if…"

"I don't need to be told I'm going to die with twisted, shrunken legs," said Hope wildly.

Booth looked away, waiting for Hope's stifled sobs to subside, then said, "What good does it do to sit out here every night, in the dark?" There was a tone of helplessness in his voice.

Hope roughly wiped the tears from her face, and looked at Booth. Her pale white face was filled with defiance. "I'm waiting for my chance," she said fiercely. "And when it comes I won't hesitate to take it."

"What chance?"

Hope turned away, her face now old and haggard looking. "That's only for me to know," she said to herself.

Isabel Chase stood quietly at the entrance to the large dining room. She wore a long silver and black satin dressing gown, making her look like a medieval queen. The only light was from two stained glass chandeliers, casting their brightness onto the long dining table. At the far end sat Addison Chase; his suit coat hanging from the back of his chair, his tie loose at his throat, and his vest unbuttoned. He stared down at his dinner plate, fork in one hand, knife in the other. His food had hardly been touched.

Isabel walked softly towards Addison. "You shouldn't be eating this late, it's not good for you."

Addison looked up, his face drawn with fatigue. "It doesn't matter," he said hoarsely, "I'm not hungry." He placed his knife and fork on the plate and pushed it away.

Isabel came up beside him, putting a hand on his shoulder. "Why are you just getting home?"

"I can't leave the office whenever I feel like it, mother."

Isabel studied him a moment. "So you leave when Brewster gives you permission?" Addison gave no reply. "How many times did he call you today?"

"I lost count," replied Addison with a weary smile.

"He's going to ruin everything if…"

"I think he already has."

"Only if you let him. Now that he has his little army of strikebreakers out there, he thinks he's in control of entire world."

"He is in control, mother."

"No. You are."

Addison got up and crossed the wide room to a set of tall French doors that faced out onto a huge stone terrace. He opened them, and took a deep breath. He spoke almost to himself. "I told him to wait—be patient. That's all we would have had to do. The miners are running out of time; out of money; and, I'm sure, out of food."

"Let me call Governor Hallgren," said Isabel, walking up behind Addison.

"No," said Addison strongly, and walked out onto the terrace.

The moon was almost full, making the shiny slate floor of the terrace glow. Addison's form looked thin and hunched in the light; like the silhouette of a frail ghost. Isabel came to him, her silver and black satin robe bright in the moonlight.

"Your father and Governor Hallgren were very good friends. He could be very useful right now."

"He'd only send in the National Guard; make this more of a mess than it is."

"There are other ways of settling things, Addison."

Addison turned and her strong, dark eyes held him. "What other ways?"

"This new coal vein you spoke of."

"The Colossal Vein?"

"If your geologist is telling the truth, and there is a fortune to be had under all that dirt, Governor Hallgren, would be interested, I'm sure. He's almost as rich as Brewster, but he wouldn't have anything against becoming richer. Plus he hates Brewster as much as Brewster hates him. I'd love to see what would happen if they went against each other."

"But you're forgetting Brewster owns the Colossal Vein."

"That means nothing. Brewster doesn't own the law. He thinks money is king, but he's a fool. The law is king. Hallgren and his cronies are the law in this state; and the money-grubbing hyenas that they control in Washington are the law. Brewster is simply a dumb dancing bear, clanging two cymbals together, compared to those people. They'd devour him."

Addison moved away into the shadows, and sat on the low stone wall bordering the terrace. He thought a moment then said, "I have to solve this myself. I can control Brewster. I have to."

"He'll cast you down into the lions den if you can't. And he'll laugh while he's doing it. I couldn't bear that."

Addison turned to her. "What makes Hallgren and his political puppets any better than Brewster, or his gutter-snipe army out there?"

"Absolutely none," answered Isabel with a smile. "Scum is scum; Republican or Democrat. But you have to make the ignorant public think there is a difference. To win out you have to make Brewster look the fool, and the villain; which is what he'll do to you if this strike gets worse."

Addison got up and walked slowly towards the house, saying, "I have no desire to become a jackal, mother."

"We shall see," said Isabel quietly.

CHAPTER 7

The sun rose red and glaring just above the horizon, slowly dissipating the low hanging mist floating a few feet above the manicured lawns of Harwick Hall. Four armed deputies moved silently through the grounds, their shotguns resting on their shoulders. They walked aimlessly, not really looking at anything; their only thoughts were to keep warm in the clinging dampness. High above them, in a huge bedroom on the second floor of the mansion, Brewster Harwick slept contentedly under a soft thick comforter; his head reclining on two large pillows.

As a shaft of sunlight reached through a window on the opposite side of the room, a delicate chiming could be heard. Brewster opened his eyes slightly, reached over to the night table beside him, and closed the lid of the solid gold pocket watch. The chiming stopped. He rolled onto his side, gave a loud, long yawn. When his eyes focused, he saw a dark form sitting across the room in a high-backed, hand carved chair. At first Brewster thought he was dreaming, but then the form took off a dirty cloth cap, bowed its head and smiled.

Brewster raised himself up on one elbow and squinted. His right hand then opened the small drawer of the night table and searched inside. The dark form held up a hand, revealing the small revolver Brewster had been after.

"What do you want?" asked Brewster, sitting up slowly, resting his back against the headboard of the bed.

As more sunlight flooded the huge room, Gentleman Jim's friendly face and grin could be seen much better. He leaned forward and tossed the revolver onto the bed. Brewster looked at it then back to Jim.

"It's still loaded," said Jim. "I trust you. Now I think you should trust me."

"Who the hell are you?"

"I work for you, Mr. Harwick. I'm from the Breakers' camp."

"How'd you get in here?"

"Wasn't all that difficult."

"Are there any guards out there?"

"Four. But their hearts don't really seem to be in it."

Brewster sat forward, agitated, his blood-red silk pajamas made him look larger than he was. He stared at Jim a moment then snatched a thick cigar from a humidor on the night table. He struck a match and puffed hard on the cigar to light it. "How'd you get here?" he asked between puffs.

"Oh, it's not much of a walk. I'm used to walking. And the moon was extremely..."

"You got a name?"

"They call me Gentleman Jim."

Brewster tossed the smoking match into a thick crystal ash tray. "How'd you come by that moniker?"

"Because I'm so polite before I do someone in."

The two men stared at each other, their faces expressionless. Finally Jim grinned. "Just funning, sir. That's one of my many faults."

"I still don't know why the hell you're here. What do you want?" asked Brewster, beginning to feel his confidence and courage returning. He reached over and picked up the revolver.

Jim watched closely and remained calm. Brewster then set the revolver on the night table.

"Thank you," said Jim. "Now to business. I've never been much of a spectator. I enjoy getting down in the mud with the rest of humanity to see what happens. You have quite a problem out there?"

"Those miners?" said Brewster. "Hell, they..."

"No, I'm talking about the Breakers you've hired. They remind me of your guards outside. They're here, but not in spirit."

"Well, I still don't know if you're here to help me or hurt me."

"Help, sir, by all means possible."

"And help yourself too, I take it?"

Jim laughed and shook a finger at Brewster. "You're a brilliant man. Yes, you are."

Brewster got up and began to pace around the room, his eyes, and Jim's, holding on one another. Brewster blew a stream of blue smoke towards the ceiling, stopped and faced Jim.

"Why do I need *you*?" asked Brewster. "I have a special police force taking care of things."

"And there's your problem. You're relying too much on law and order."

Brewster started to grin, but suppressed it. "And you have a better way?"

"A smart man doesn't sweat when he works. Only plow horses and jackasses sweat when they work. And that's exactly what you have at the Breakers' camp. They've never had it this good in their miserable, rat-infested lives."

"I thought you were one of them?"

"For the moment," replied Jim. "You see I've always been interested in the next step. Those people out there are only interested in momentary pleasures. A pocket full of dimes sends them into ecstasy. But luckily, I'm able to see further than that."

"Now we're getting somewhere," said Brewster, crossing back to his bed and sitting. He pulled the drawer of the night table open wider, and brought out six neatly bound packets of hundred dollar bills. He shook one of the packets at Jim. "Know how much is here?"

"No, sir."

"A thousand dollars. Ever had a thousand dollars at one time?"

"Never."

"You'd like this, wouldn't you?"

"I certainly wouldn't refuse it."

"Then quit beating around the proverbial bush and tell me what you can do for me."

"End the strike."

"When and how?"

"Soon. And with both sides bringing about the end."

"You can do this?"

"I've no doubt about it. A little money now, and a little later, is all that's required."

"When can you make this happen?"

"Tomorrow night should be a good beginning."

Brewster tossed the packet of money at Jim's feet. Jim glanced at it, his face stony with resentment; feeling like a dog who had just been thrown a scrap of meat.

"Go on, take it," said Brewster. "Let me see what you can do with it. I'm beginning to like you, Gentleman Jim."

Jim leaned down, picked up the money, and put it in his coat pocket. "I won't disappoint you," he said, smiling.

Brewster went to the other side of the room to a large desk. He sat down and turned on a lamp. "Come over here."

Jim walked leisurely to the front of the desk. Brewster shoved a black object towards him. It was mounted on a shiny brass pedestal. Jim then saw it was a large lump of coal.

Brewster smiled. "Watch," he said, and slowly turned the piece of coal around in the lamp light. One side of it looked exactly like a finely cut diamond. Jim stared in amazement, his mouth slightly open. The coal even sparkled like a diamond.

"What do you think?" asked Brewster, grinning proudly.

"Shines like nothing I've ever seen," answered Jim. "Is it fake?"

"Hell, no, it's real. Ten years ago an old miner, who worked in the coal field here, brought it to me. Never seen anything like it since— neither has anyone else."

Brewster's face took on a child-like quality as he stared at his black diamond. "Sometimes, before I go to bed, I sit here and stare at it. And I remember these black rocks are better than diamonds; worth more than diamonds. Coal runs the world, not diamonds. It runs the furnaces of the factories, the boilers of the office buildings, the trains. It heats millions of homes. Yes, these little black beauties are worth more than any diamond on earth."

"And make men like you very, very rich," said Jim.

Brewster looked at Jim a moment. "You dream much, Gentleman Jim?"

Jim gave a quick grunt. "I'm afraid when you're on the road, you don't have much time for dreaming. Unless it's about food and a warm place to sleep."

"I dream about being rich. Richer than the Vanderbilts, the Rockefellers, or anyone else in this goddamn world."

"That's going to take quite a lot of money, sir."

"It'll happen. I'll make it happen."

"I believe you can. But be careful morals don't get in your way. It's a terrible stumbling block."

Brewster laughed loudly and sat back in his chair. He studied Jim closely, and puffed on his cigar. "I think we'll do fine, Gentleman Jim."

"So do I, sir."

"Only don't cross me, I can be a dangerous dog."

"Can't we all, when we howl with the wolves."

"You like that thousand I just gave you?"

"Love it like pie."

"There'll be more if you get my mine back quick."

"It's not a problem."

"What do you intend to do?"

"Stir up the life force. Make things happen. Bring things to the boiling point."

"Then get to it."

"I'm on my way, sir," said Jim with a slight bow, and slapped his grimy cap onto his head.

———

The sun was higher now, dazzling white, and burning away the valley mist. The motionless humid air warned of the coming heat of the day.

Addison Chase moved briskly down the long staircase from the second floor of his house. He was dressed in a freshly pressed gray suit and vest, starched white shirt, black tie and shiny black shoes. He carried a stylish gray fedora hat in one hand. As he opened the front door of the entrance hall, his chauffeur and touring car were already waiting for him at the foot of the stone stairs.

"You're not having breakfast with me?" called Isabel.

Addison turned and saw his mother standing in the doorway of the dinning room. She was wearing a rose-pink dress trimmed in white silk that reached to her ankles. Her white, patent leather shoes matched the brilliance of the dress.

"I'll get some breakfast in Palmyra, mother," replied Addison.

"At least have some warm milk and honey before you go, it'll do your stomach good."

"Thank you, mother, but I need to get to the office."

The telephone, off to one corner of the entrance hall, began ringing and Addison walked towards it.

"Let Elinor answer it," said Isabel.

"I think I can manage it," said Addison, picking up the receiver. "Addison, here. Yes, Brewster, I'm already on my way in to see how things are going."

Isabel went into the dining room, crossed to a far door, and entered a huge, high-ceilinged library. At a small desk was a telephone extension. She delicately picked up the receiver and put it to her ear.

"And you're no longer to make any more decisions on this strike without consulting me first," said Brewster.

"I've only tried to do what..." began Addison.

"You've been handling this all wrong from the beginning," interrupted Brewster. "I kept telling you that. These Breakers are stalling, and it's costing me thousands of dollars a day. And that halfwit Deets just stands around watching them."

"There have already been people killed," said Addison. "How many more do..."

"As many as it takes. You don't do anything more till you hear from me. That clear?"

"If that's what you want, Brewster."

"You and Deets are turning into a couple of weak fish, and I don't like it."

"Now wait a minute, Brewster, Deets and I are trying to keep this thing from blowing up in all our faces."

"Well, Deets might not have to worry about that if I get rid of him. And you might not have a job much longer either."

There was a loud click at the other end of the line. Addison stood there stunned. His face grew pale and clammy despite the sweat on his forehead. He slowly hung up the receiver, then felt someone beside him.

"He's planning to force you out," said Isabel coldly, her face as pale as Addison's. "And all your hard work and sacrifices will have been for nothing—all your father's hard work that made Harwick Coal a giant. Don't be a slave to that savage. It's time for you to take what's rightfully yours."

"Brewster's a powerful man," said Addison softly.

"So is Governor Hallgren. Let me call Langdon and have a chat with him."

Addison sat down in a chair beside the telephone, took out a handkerchief from his coat pocket, and wiped the sweat from his forehead and upper lip.

"Why do you keep insisting Brewster's a powerful man?" asked Isabel.

"Money. The power of money. Sometimes I think it can even raise the dead."

Isabel got down on her knees and looked at Addison with intense, penetrating eyes. "You're the one who deserves to control Harwick Coal. Only you."

"And how will that miracle happen?"

"We'll make it happen. You just have to believe in yourself, like I believe in you. You control Harwick Coal right now. Never forget that."

"What could Hallgren do?"

Isabel smiled. "I'll show you."

Gentleman Jim, Handsome, and Oracle came walking casually down the main road away from the Breakers' camp. Two deputies sat on the running board of one of the two dump trucks that still blocked the entire road. They waited calmly, their shotguns across their knees, watching the three approach.

"Where you boys think you're goin'?" asked one of the deputies, and spit a long stream of tobacco juice into the deep powdery dust of the road.

"Going to be another hot day, looks like," answered Jim, taking off his cap and wiping the sweat from his balding head.

"You didn't answer the man's question," said the second deputy, and clicked the safety of his shotgun to "off".

"I apologize," said Jim with a nod. "There's not much going on in camp, so my friends and I thought we might be able to hitch a ride into Palmyra when you…"

"You three monkeys head on back where you came from," said the first deputy, and spit another stream of tobacco juice—this time towards Jim.

Jim and Handsome glanced at the brown streak in the dust, then looked at the deputy as if deciding whether to kill him now or later. Oracle simply stood there with a friendly grin on his face.

"Any of you bunch go near Palmyra," continued the first deputy, "you'll be arrested and escorted to the county line—head first or feet first, it don't matter to us."

"I didn't know," said Jim politely. "I'm sorry. Thank you for the information. We'll go right back to camp then."

"That would be the smart thing to do," said the second deputy.

"Going to be a hot one," said Jim, walking away, followed by Handsome and Oracle.

"Yeah, yeah, go on," said the first deputy.

The three hadn't gone but a few yards when a small Chevy coupe appeared on the road, coming from the direction of mine seven. The auto's brakes gave a weak screeching sound as it came to stop near the road block. The deputies got up from the running board of the dump truck and walked forward.

"Morning, fellas, morning," said Roscoe Brodie, leaning his head out the driver's window, a wide grin on his face. "Glad to see you again."

The deputies remained a few feet from Brodie, their shotguns resting on their shoulders. "Insurance man," said the first deputy. "I thought they'd of kicked your ass out long ago."

"How much money did you make, insurance man?" said the other deputy, and gave a quick laugh.

"Now don't rag on me fellas, I made a lot of good contacts at that old mine. Good prospects every one."

"The hell with that," said the first deputy. "What'd you see up there? You said you'd have some information for us."

"Well," began Brodie, scratching his head, "truth to tell, didn't see much, didn't hear much. They didn't let me move around like I thought they might."

As Brodie continued talking, Handsome took a couple steps forward and stared.

Jim looked from Handsome to Brodie, asking, "What is it?"

"That lug in the car," answered Handsome, still watching Brodie. "He was at that meeting last night. He's the union fella I told you about."

Jim's expression turned troubled. "This isn't good at all," he said quietly.

"Oh, no," said Oracle sadly.

Jim and Handsome looked at Oracle, and saw him pointing to the left front tire of Brodie's auto; it was starting to go flat.

"You're beginning to irritate me, insurance man," said the first deputy. "We let you go in there cause you said you'd find out things."

"You ain't found out diddley," said the other deputy.

"Easy, fellas, easy," replied Brodie, holding up a hand. "I didn't say I was done, did I?"

"What the hell's that mean?" asked the first deputy.

"I can go on back in there bright and early tomorrow. Do some more talking; get a better look around. Then I can…"

"You can shut up," said the second deputy.

"You ain't goin' nowhere but down the damn road, flannel mouth," said the first deputy, motioning with his thumb.

"And right now," said the other deputy, pointing his shotgun at Brodie.

"I hate to interrupt," said Jim politely.

The deputies, and Brodie, looked and saw Jim, Handsome, and Oracle standing a few feet away.

"I told you monkeys to move on out of here," said the first deputy, and lowered his shotgun at them.

"Yes, I remember," said Jim, bowing his head, "but there's that tire there."

The deputies looked, and Brodie leaned his head out of the window.

"I got a flat?" asked Brodie.

"Not to worry," said Jim, "you have some good Samaritans right here."

"You might know I'd have my best bib and tucker on," said Brodie, shaking his head.

"Just sit there, sir," said Jim.

"Get this jalopy out of here," said the first deputy angrily.

"There's a perfect spot just down the road," said Jim, pointing to a brushy, tree-shaded area. "If you'll allow us, we'll…"

"Go on," said the second deputy with a jerk of his thumb.

"Hang on, sir," said Jim to Brodie, as he, Handsome, and Oracle pushed the small coupe between the two dump trucks, and on down the road, and off to the right side, behind a tangled wall of wiry brush and weeds.

Brodie opened the tiny trunk of the coupe and took out the jack and handle. Handsome carried the spare tire to the front of the auto.

"Let my friend do that," said Jim, taking off his cap and swatting the dust and dead leaves from the top of a decayed tree stump. "Sit here, make yourself comfortable."

Brodie handed the jack and handle to Handsome, walked over into the shade, and sat on the stump. He began fanning himself with his straw hat. "I sure appreciate this, fellas," he said. "I ain't got much money on me, but how's fifty cents sound for your trouble?"

"No, no," replied Jim. "As I said, we're good Samaritans."

"Like in the Bible," said Oracle. He was seated cross-legged in the dirt, right in front of Brodie, and staring at him.

Jim remained standing, his back resting against a tree, only a few feet from Brodie.

"I heard the deputy say you're in the insurance business," said Jim.

"That's right," said Brodie, turning his head to Jim.

"Any on yourself?"

"Not miners' insurance," said Brodie with a smile. "Got some life though. Smart thing to have, I think."

"Yes. Never know when something's going to go wrong."

"How true, my friend, how true."

Suddenly, Brodie began to feel uncomfortable under Jim's steady gaze. He looked at Oracle, whose large round eyes were studying him, unblinkingly. Brodie continued fanning himself with his hat, watching Handsome change the tire. Handsome stopped, looked at Brodie, smiled and winked, then went back to work.

Brodie turned to Jim with a nervous smile. "You…you fellas must be from over there at the camp?"

Jim gave an embarrassed nod. "Guilty, sir."

"Rough bunch, I'll bet."

"Children of the Devil," said Oracle.

Brodie started to laugh, but stopped when he saw how serious Oracle was.

Jim stepped a little ways from the tree, making Brodie turn his back to Oracle. "One has to learn how to play the game with people like that," said Jim.

"Game?" said Brodie.

"The great game," replied Jim. "From the day we're born till the day we die. Even when the days stink like rotten meat."

Brodie quit fanning himself. He didn't know why, but he rose slowly; something in him told him to run, but he hesitated.

"How you doing there, Handsome?" asked Jim in a friendly voice.

"One more minute," answered Handsome cheerfully.

For several seconds, there was absolute silence, then, in the distance, came the happy singing of a meadow lark. Oracle got quickly to his feet, causing Brodie to flinch noticeably.

"Ignore him, sir," said Jim. "He's always been excitable as a fly."

"I wish I could whistle like that," said Oracle, his eyes closed tightly, lost in the song of the lone bird; his lips pursed together, moving slightly as if whistling the same song.

"I...I think I better be getting on, fellas," said Brodie.

The dark, hungry look of Jim's eyes made Brodie turn and hurry to his auto. Handsome tossed the tire jack to one side and stood up, blocking the driver's side door.

"Don't rush off," said Jim, following. "We don't mean you any harm."

"Or any good," said Handsome, flashing that charming smile of his.

"Now, Handsome," said Jim, walking up and putting a foot on the running board of the coupe, "you keep that rascally humor of yours to yourself."

"I think I have fleas," said Oracle, coming around from the rear of the auto, scratching his head violently.

Brodie found himself surrounded. He thrust his hand into his trouser pocket. "Here...here's that fifty cents I promised."

"You know what's fascinating, Mr. Insurance Man?" said Jim. "Most people would rather face a starving wolf than the truth."

"Truth?" said Brodie weakly.

"That time can't be stopped, and death won't wait for any one."

Jim held out his arm, fist clenched. Brodie held out the fifty cent piece to him, but Jim's thumb went up straight, and was slowly turned towards the ground. Oracle grabbed Brodie and snapped his neck. Brodie dropped to the ground like a wet rag.

Walking cautiously to the edge of the main road, Jim looked towards the deputies at the road block. They were seated on the opposite side of one of the dump trucks, on the wide running board, unaware of what had happened. Handsome and Oracle stuffed Brodie's body, head-first, into the small trunk of the coupe.

"Hide the car well, Handsome," said Jim, walking back to them. "Then come to camp soon as you can. Oracle, you help him."

"I did good, huh, Jim?" asked Oracle.

"You did excellent."

Grinning proudly, Oracle helped Handsome and Jim push the coupe on down the main road. Handsome got in the driver's seat, and Oracle in the passenger's. Jim quickly returned to the cover of the trees and tall brush. After coasting as far as they could, Handsome started the auto and drove away.

As the morning wore on, many of the women of mine seven began making their way to the company store. Small groups of thin, dirty-faced children accompanied them. The women were dressed in flimsy summer dresses of faded white or gray; a few had checkered ribbon around the edges of the sleeves. Handmade bows and hip sashes adorned some of the others, trying to make the dresses less drab and worn-looking. Most of the boy children were shirtless, wearing only thread-bare, knee-length pants, and were barefooted. The girl children, also barefooted, wore plain cotton dresses with the badly frayed hems hanging below their knees.

The outside and inside of the company store was a dismal representation of a general store. No paint had been applied for years, and the front steps and porch sagged from neglect and heavy foot traffic. The interior walls were covered with shelves, floor to ceiling; every square foot of space being used to display over-priced goods of all kinds. Running down the center of the huge store were long wooden tables piled high with work shirts and work pants, piles of work boots, women's and children's shoes. There were hats and caps for men, and a few for women and children. Here and there fat wooden barrels held picks, shovels, sledge hammers, and spare handles for each. A few tall windows stood open, letting in a rush of warm air now and then, along with just enough sunlight to see from one end of the gloomy building to the other.

On the far side of the room was a short wooden counter with a scarred top and hand-cranked, tinny cash register setting in the middle. The proprietor, Jacob Zweig, leaned on the counter top, with both elbows, studying an accounts ledger, and mumbling softly as if memorizing it. He glanced up for a moment when the women and children began filing in through the main door. He grunted disgustedly, and went back to the ledger. His fat, unshaven face was shiny with sweat, his short fat body hung heavy against the edge of the counter. His puffy arms bulged from the sweaty short-sleeved shirt he wore.

"Don't have much can goods on the shelf, Zweig," said one of the women.

"That's because I ain't got much can goods," replied Zweig, without looking up.

"Mama," said a young child, her bangs hanging down to her eyebrows as she stared with bright eyes at a large glass bowl of lemon drops. "Can I have some, please?"

"Not right now, angel," replied the mother.

"Just a penny for three," said the child.

"Can't live on candy, girl."

The child remained staring at the sugar-coated lemon drops, while the mother's eyes searched the wide, half-empty food shelves.

"The Lord will provide. He will provide." The six-foot-tall, lanky, wrinkled woman kept repeating the words as she walked among the tables, clutching a tattered, limp Bible in her hands. She never looked at anything, she just walked, saying, "The Lord will provide."

Some of the smaller children began crawling around under the tables, chasing each other, giggling, and having fun.

Zweig watched the squirming children, disapprovingly, with his round watery eyes. "Hey," he said sharply, "you're not at home now, you wild Indians."

The children stopped and stared at him, not sure what to do.

"Mr. Zweig," said a small, meek woman with glasses, "do you have any apples left?"

Zweig looked at her with raised eyebrows, then at the frail, bony woman she was helping to the counter.

"My mother wanted to make some apple sauce," said the woman with the glasses. "Just a little bit."

"A little I ain't got," replied Zweig harshly, then slammed his ledger closed. "But you know what I got? Plenty of nothing."

"Zweig, you ornery old crocodile, we need groceries," said a heavy set woman, walking up to Zweig, unintimidated. "You're holding back on us, ain't you?"

The other women agreed, and Zweig stood up as tall as his squat little frame could reach, and folded his arms tightly across his chest.

"You got complaints?" he said. "See Morgan McAlister. He gave me orders."

"About what?" asked a woman from the far side of the store.

"Rationing. From now on," replied Zweig. "No hording of food, no making pigs of yourselves. You get so much a day. And I write it down here." He slapped his ledger. "You got complaints, see Morgan McAlister."

"What you got in the back?" asked another woman. "You must have more than this."

"I must have?" said Zweig, eyebrows raised, eyes hostile. "Well, I would have, if someone hadn't started a strike. So now we can watch each other starve."

"Shut your mouth, you old gargoyle," said a woman, angrily. "My kids ain't going to starve."

"So it's my fault what happened?" replied Zweig, just as angry.

"It's the Devil," said the tall, lanky woman, holding her Bible high. "The Devil has come among us."

"Shut up, Mary," said a woman behind her.

"Yah, yah," said Zweig in disgust, "now I'm the Devil, too." He walked towards the other end of the store, trying to get away from the converging women.

"So what are we allowed?" asked a woman, frowning with worry.

"So much a day," answered Zweig. "Two cups of flour, one cup of beans, a little coffee, a slice of salt pork, or two slices of smoked bacon."

"That's all?" said an old woman.

"I have sardines, anchovies. One tin for each customer, and a little smoked herring."

"How the hell we supposed to live on that?" said a woman, stepping directly in from of Zweig.

"It's not my fault. It's the strike committee. A little each day is what you get."

"Until we starve?"

Zweig shrugged and looked away.

"I don't see any canned milk," said a young woman, holding a tiny baby in her arms. "My baby needs it."

Zweig came back along the counter to her. "There's no milk. There won't be any. Mr. Chase won't let any supplies in till the strike ends. I'm innocent."

"So's the Devil," said another woman.

"I only run the store. I'm paid a few pennies a day, and allowed to live in the back. I don't even have a house to..."

"Excuse me while I wipe away my tears," said a woman.

Zweig was about to make an angry reply, but instead grabbed his ledger book and disappeared into a back storeroom, cursing under his breath.

"What about tobacco for my pipe?" yelled a short, grizzled woman.

"Tobacco's all gone," Zweig yelled without turning.

"Well, girls," said a stoop-shouldered, fat woman, "let's all pray Mr. Roscoe Brodie lives up to his promises."

"He said he'd help us," said the woman next to her. "Said he could bring in union people; run the strikebreakers off."

"When?" asked another woman. "How long before he comes?"

"We've got to support our men," said another woman, strongly. "We can't have any doubts, any fears. We've got to keep our families together. We have to endure."

"That's all fine, Muriel," said a woman, leaning tiredly against the counter, "but we can't eat endurance. My two kids had to share a piece of bread for breakfast. I'm out of everything."

"When you're out of money, you're out of everything," chimed in one of the women.

"And that won't be too damn long, I can tell you," replied the woman at the counter.

"How long can we go on with a cup of beans and a slice of bacon?" asked a woman.

"And how long before our old people take sick and start dying?"

"If the strike goes into winter," said a woman, "how do we buy shoes?"

"You don't need shoes when you're in the graveyard," said the tall, lanky woman with the Bible.

All the women turned to her, and so did the children.

"Ah, quit your babbling, Mary," said a woman. "That's all you do with that Bible of yours. Can't you find some goods things in there to say?"

Mary stood near one of the tall open windows, the sunlight behind her; her stick figure a black silhouette in the bright light. A hot breeze swept in, and her thin, loose dress billowed out like a shroud. Her long, gray hair streamed in the direction of the women as she looked down and opened her Bible. "And when the fourth seal was opened, a voice, like thunder, said, 'Come. And behold there came a pale horse, and its rider's name was Death; with the power to kill with sword, famine, pestilence, and wild beasts of the earth'."

The young woman, who had asked for canned milk for her baby, picked up a shoe from one of the tables, ready to throw it, but stopped when Mary raised the Bible into the air. A rasping gush of wind rushed through the open window, and the thin, tattered pages fluttered loudly—like the wings of a startled dove.

CHAPTER 8

The morning train from Palmyra arrived in Columbus, Ohio just before noon. Addison and Isabel Chase took a cab to the State Capitol, where they were to have a private luncheon with Governor Langdon Hallgren, and his aide Hugh Underhill.

Governor Hallgren, dressed in a very expensive suit, vest and tie, was a tall muscular man with curly, snow-white hair; his face was lean and pale looking. He had the keen, prominent eyes of a predator. He walked with one arm around Addison, and the other around Isabel. Hugh Underhill followed, smiling. He was an impressive, athletic type, his face smooth and finely molded. His hair was dark brown and combed in precise wavy layers. He was extremely alert, concerned only with the Governor's demands and prosperity, which aided in his prosperity. He never fawned over the Governor, or licked his boots as they say. Underhill was also a predator.

"You haven't aged a day since I last saw you, Isabel," said Hallgren in his strong, gravelly voice. His teeth showed bright white as he smiled.

"Nor you, Langdon," replied Isabel, deeply flattered.

"And Addison," Hallgren went on, "you always did remind me of your father. What a friend he was, I'll never forget him."

"Thank you, Langdon," said Addison. "He always said the best about you."

"Come on, let's eat, I'm starving." Hallgren led them through the open double doors to a small, but fancy dining room.

The black walnut dining table shone under the lights of the crystal chandelier, and the plush, red velvet dining chairs were trimmed in gold brocade. The emerald green carpeting was thick and soft, and soothing to walk on.

Two negro men, wearing starched white jackets and trousers, white gloves and red bow ties, stood at one end of the table. They each moved quickly, drawing back a chair, and assisted Isabel and Addison to sit, then they did the same for Hallgren and Underhill.

"You may serve now, Clayton," said Hallgren to one of the men.

Clayton motioned to the other man who hurried to the far end of the room, opened another set of double doors, and signaled to his right. Seconds later, two negro women, all in white—shoes, dresses, aprons, gloves and caps, appeared with a large gold serving cart.

"You've got to start coming to the captiol more often, Isabel," began Hallgren. "We're growing impressively here. We've got just as good restaurants, theaters, and hotels as any where."

"I know, Langdon," said Isabel, spreading her embroidered linen napkin across her lap. "But things have taken an unsettling turn where we are."

"I know. We've been keeping an eye on the situation. Right, Hugh?"

"Yes. It's getting somewhat violent the last we heard," replied Underhill, and looked at Addison. "Is it going to get any worse, you think?"

"Not if some changes are made," said Addison confidently. "But it will have to be done soon."

"Good," said Hallgren, and waited for the two negro maids to finish setting the luncheon plates, and glasses of iced water on the table.

Clayton and the other man stepped quickly to the table and removed the sterling silver warming covers from each of the large plates.

"Thank you, Clayton," said Hallgren. "I'll ring if we need anything more."

"Yes, Governor."

Clayton gave a swift flick of his hand towards the double doors. The two women hurried out with the serving cart, followed by Clayton and his assistant, who silently closed the doors behind them.

"I hope you don't have any objections to prime rib, Isabel?" said Hallgren, picking up his knife and fork. "My chef is a genius. And I had him add his specialty of asparagus and creamed potatoes."

"It looks magnificent, Langdon," replied Isabel.

"Hope it's not too bloody for you, but I can't stand burnt meat," said Hallgren with a shudder.

"It's perfect," said Underhill, chewing on a large juicy piece.

"So, Addison," began Hallgren, carving into his thick slab of beef, "when your mother telephoned, she mentioned a golden opportunity that needs some assistance."

"A colossal opportunity," said Isabel with a smile, and dipped a piece of bread into the bloody juice on her plate.

Addison glanced at Isabel, amused by her reference to the Colossal coal vein. "To be correct, the golden opportunity is really black."

"I don't follow," said Hallgren, frowning.

"A new coal vein has been discovered at mine seven. There hasn't been anything like it here in America, and may never be again. And I don't think Brewster Harwick is the man to control it."

Hallgren stopped chewing and stared at Addison a moment. "What is this new vein worth?"

"Astronomical," replied Addison, still not having touched his food. "It could put Brewster right up there along side Carnegie and Rockefeller."

Hallgren and Underhill glanced at one another, set their knives and forks down, and gave their undivided attention to Addison.

Isabel covered her smile of satisfaction with her napkin, then moved her plate away, preparing to control the meeting if need be.

"How sure are you about all this?" asked Hallgren.

"Very sure," said Addison. "I've brought all the geologist's reports and maps with me. I think you should have a look at them before we leave."

"But this strike," said Underhill, "it's turned into a pretty bloody game. Don't you have any control?"

"I did. But now Brewster has decided he knows better."

Hallgren gave a short, guttural laugh. "Well, that doesn't surprise me."

"But what's in the hearts of those men?" asked Underhill.

"What men?" said Addison, not understanding.

"The miners. How determined are they?"

Addison shrugged. "They've already proved they're willing to die."

"Not good," said Hallgren. "I could send in the National Guard tomorrow, but I won't. I'd love to see Brewster get so deep in this that every newspaper in the country would write what a greedy rat he really is."

"I'll second that," said Isabel.

"On my run for a second term," said Hallgren, "he put up two hundred thousand dollars, hoping my opponent would defeat me. Did you know that?"

"Why no," said Isabel, shocked. She looked at Addison.

"Absolutely not," said Addison. "He never said a word to me." He looked at Isabel, deeply worried that the meeting was now headed for failure.

"If we'd have known, Langdon," said Isabel, "we would have warned you."

"I know, I know," replied Hallgren, picking up his knife and fork. "I'm not blaming you or Addison."

"You've got some law enforcement there in Palmyra," said Underhill. "What are they doing about the strike?"

"Nothing," said Addison. "Sheriff Deets is like a beached whale. The strikebreakers are the ones in control. But I agree with you on not sending in the National Guard. Not yet."

"Obviously, you came here with a plan," said Underhill. "Is it a good one?"

"If we can get Brewster out of the way," replied Addison, and finally began eating.

"When you grab a wolf by the ears," said Hallgren, "you'd better not let go."

"I have no intention of grabbing Brewster's ears," said Addison. "Before we left Palmyra, I realized what the key to all this is."

"And what is this key?" asked Hallgren.

"Abigail Harwick."

"His wife?" said Underhill. "I think I met her once. At a dinner party in Chicago. Very beautiful woman."

"And very lonely," said Isabel. "And very, very unhappy. Has been for a long time."

"And how is Mrs. Harwick a key?" asked Hallgren, ignoring his lunch again.

"Half of Brewster's property is in her name?" answered Addison.

Hallgren and Underhill couldn't help smiling.

"Are you sure?" asked Hallgren.

"Yes."

"How sure?" asked Underhill.

"I helped draw up the papers," replied Addison. "It was years ago, when Brewster had just taken over everything from his father. He was more interested in the money, not the headaches of running an empire. He was doing things, and making investments that could have gotten him into a lot of trouble. So I talked him into putting a large amount of his property in Abigail's name. That way he wouldn't lose too much if things went wrong; and he could continue in his wild ways."

"And this…this Colossal vein is hers?" asked Hallgren.

"Every piece of coal, and every penny it'll bring in," said Addison.

"Does she know this?" asked Underhill.

"No. She was like Brewster in the beginning; only concerned about the money, and the glory and the glamour."

"Do you think you can control her?" said Hallgren.

"It shouldn't be too difficult," said Addison, and glanced at Isabel. "My mother and Abigail have grown very close over the years."

"I have a distinct feeling," began Isabel, "that Abigail would be more than happy to make Brewster as miserable as he's made her."

"I've got one more year before my term is up," said Hallgren. "I'd just as soon retire from politics and enjoy the fruits of my labor. But what is it you're asking of me exactly?"

"Help me take control of Harwick Coal," replied Addison. "The rest I don't care about—the lumber mills, the cattle ranches—they're just needless headaches."

Hallgren studied Addison long and hard before he spoke. "You sure you can do this?"

"With you I can," said Addison.

"With your contacts in Washington and Wall Street, it'll be child's play," added Isabel. "You've done it before. You own the state legislature."

"Well, all that aside," said Hallgren cautiously, "I'll have to make some telephone calls first; see what certain people think about this. How this can be done swiftly and discreetly. You know, Addison, I'm beginning to see your father in you more and more. He lived to make money; enjoyed the power—like the rest of us. I'm impressed with you."

"Thank you, Langdon."

"What do you think of all this, Hugh?" Hallgren asked.

"Anything is possible," replied Underhill. "But Abigail Harwick has to come over to us. And remain under our control."

"I don't think that will be a problem," said Isabel.

Underhill turned to Hallgren, saying, "We could put pressure on Harwick right now through the railroads, and the coal brokers in Chicago, New York, and Philadelphia."

"Might be too soon for that," answered Hallgren.

"What kind of pressure?" asked Addison.

"Certain rail lines could raise the freight rates to move Harwick coal," said Underhill. "And certain influencial coal brokers could refuse to buy Harwick coal. If the brokers have too much coal on hand already, why would they pay Harwick anything?"

"I like it," said Addison, smiling for the first time. "I think it should be done now."

"Yes, I think it's brilliant," said Isabel.

"And that would just be the opening gambit," said Underhill, pleased with himself. "There are endless possibilities. But we need to get Harwick in a very tight corner. One he can't get out of."

"But understand, this all has to be done for the good of the people," said Hallgren. "If Brewster if oppressing the hopes and dreams of the workingman, it's our duty to step in and stop him."

"We'd have no choice in the matter," said Underhill.

"We'll need absolute power," said Addison.

"The congress and senate, here, do as I suggest they do," replied Hallgren.

"And certain friends in the congress and senate, in Washington, are just as accommodating," added Underhill. "Is that the kind of power you were referring to?"

"Exactly," said Addison.

"And those who can't be bribed," said Hallgren, "can be blackmailed. There are always skeletons in someone's closet. Lackeys and stooges are a dime a dozen. Brewster is only one man; he's humpty dumpty sitting on a wall."

"This has been such a perfect lunch, Langdon," said Isabel. "How can we ever thank you enough?"

"It's been my pleasure, Isabel. Now, precisely how many millions of dollars does this Colossal vein have in it?"

CHAPTER 9

They moved swiftly and silently through the darkness. In two hours the sun would be up. Handsome seemed to have the eyes of a cat as he rushed in and out among the trees and the shallow drainage ditches. Oracle held tight to the hem of Handsome's coat, watching every move he made. They each clutched a small round can of kerosene under one arm—each can wrapped tightly with a burlap bag. If the cans were dropped accidentaly there would be no sound.

Handsome stopped to rest, and peered into the surrounding blackness, listening intently. Oracle leaned in close, squinting at Handsome's face.

"What's wrong, Handsome?"

"Nothing," whispered Handsome. "Everything's fine. Don't talk unless you have to."

"Where are we?" asked Oracle softly.

"We're almost there," said Handsome, putting a finger to his lips.

Oracle did the same, like a child promising to be very quiet.

All the houses of mine seven were dark and silent. There were the usual guards walking up and down the main street, and some of the alley ways. Other guards were posted around the mine and its buildings. Out of the stillness of the night the only sounds were from high up near the mine itself; the dull throbbing of the water pumps, drawing the hot water from the bottom of the deep shafts, and the muffled roar of the huge exhaust fans, expelling the poisoned gases from the tunnels and gangways.

The community hall was dark, but the windows stood open to the humid air. Handsome and Oracle crept to a corner of the building and sat down, their backs resting against the weathered boards. Handsome looked cautiously around, then spoke softly.

"You remember what to do?"

"Yes."

"You sure?"

"I never forget anything Jim tells me. But I would feel better if he were here."

"He had to go see a man. Get some more money for us; like before. You saw all that money Jim got."

"That was good."

"Well, Jim went to get some more. We're going to be rich."

"But will we be happy or sad?"

"We'll be having too hell of a good time to notice," said Handsome. "You got your matches?"

"A whole box," said Oracle, reaching into his coat pocket.

"Wait here, quiet as a mouse."

"A tiny mouse."

Handsome started to move away and Oracle grabbed him.

"I...I don't like being alone in the dark, Handsome."

"I'll only be a minute. Then we'll go back. Be with Jim."

"Good, good," said Oracle, smiling and nodding.

Within seconds, Handsome was gone, and the silence closed in around Oracle. He grew afraid and pressed the can of kerosene to his chest for protection.

Handsome had only traveled thirty yards from the community hall to the side of the company store. The windows stood open like those of the community hall. Handsome crawled in without a sound. He struck a match and it sputtered to life. Holding the dim flame before him, he moved to the center of the store, his sharp eyes taking in as much as he could of the surrounding shelves and tables. That beautiful, engaging smile of his appeared when he saw bottle after bottle of rubbing alcohol crowding three entire shelves, then the match went out. Handsome knelt down, opened the can of kerosene and let it pour across the dry wooden floor. He stood up and began taking the bottles of alcohol and smashing them against the side of the cash register counter—bottle after bottle. The smile never left his face until a light went on in a back room, on the far side of the store. Handsome quickly struck a match, let it burn a few seconds, and set it gently on the floor. The kerosene and alcohol began to flame slowly.

Jacob Zweig came out of the small back room dressed in a thin nightshirt, half-asleep, and watery-eyed as usual. He reached for a light switch on the wall then saw yellow and blue flames wandering across the floor. His eyes grew wide in fright, his mouth opened, but he only uttered a startled grunt as Handsome's knife plunged into the center of his back.

Oracle was twisting and turning, looking one way then another, but all around him was only blackness. A dog barked in the distance and he stopped moving, wondering if the dog had smelled him. Suddenly someone was beside him. He started to cry out when a hand went over his mouth.

"It's me," said Handsome in a frantic whisper. "Hurry up, dump that kerosene."

Oracle stood up and emptied his can of kerosene down the inside wall of the community hall. Handsome looked in the direction of the company store. There was just the hint of rising flames through one of the windows near the front door.

"This isn't working right," said Oracle calmly, but disappointed.

Handsome grabbed the box of matches from him, struck four at one time and dropped them to the floor. The kerosene caught fire and the flames began to spread.

Holding tight to Handsome's coattail again, Oracle was led back in the direction they had come from. They hadn't gone far when Handsome stumbled and fell, and Oracle landed hard on top of him. Both couldn't help letting out a surprised grunt.

"Who's that?" said a man's voice.

Handsome and Oracle didn't move. Handsome whispered into Oracle's ear then got up.

"It's only me," said Handsome.

"Who the hell is me?" asked the voice.

Handsome and Oracle stood waiting as the black form of a man with a rifle walked up.

"Morgan McAlister sent me," said Handsome.

"Sent you to do what?"

"Now, Oracle," said Handsome quietly, and snatched the man's rifle from him.

Oracle's thick arms were around the man's neck in seconds, and there was a sharp, sickening snap.

Brewster Harwick lay on his side, sleeping contentedly on top his cool white sheets, his head nestled in the center of a thick soft pillow. He snored loudly, and there was a slight trickle of drool from the corner of his mouth. He was naked, and the revolving ceiling fan helped cool his large, hairy bulk.

The windows of his bedroom were all open and an army of crickets could be heard chirping. The dark room suddenly filled with a loud ringing. Startled, Brewster rolled onto his back, giving several loud snorts from his open mouth. His hand groped for the telephone on the night table beside him.

"What?" he said, still half asleep. Within a few seconds he sat up, listening intently to the voice on the other end of the line. He switched on the lamp near the telephone, and gradually a smile came to his face. "Did it spread to the houses?" The smile faded. "Any idea how it started?" he asked, rubbing his eyes then jerked his head up. "The mine's all right, isn't it? Good, good. You tell Booth McAlister, if anything happens to the mine, I'm holding him responsible—and he can pack his goddamn suitcase and get out. Fine, Addison, call me later if you find out anything more." He slammed the telephone down. "Wake me up for that," he grumbled. "Christ."

He heard a faint chiming from the far side of the room, glanced at the night table and saw his gold pocket watch was missing. At that instant a lamp went on at the large desk across the room. Gentleman Jim could be seen sitting behind the desk, the pocket watch in his hand. He was smiling as he listened to the gentle, soothing chiming.

"I couldn't help admiring this the first time I was here," said Jim earnestly.

Brewster reached behind him and draped a sheet over himself. "How the hell do you get in here?" he said loudly.

"It's not that difficult."

"You're going to give me a goddamn heart attack," said Brewster, getting up and wrapping the sheet clear around himself.

Jim smiled as he watched Brewster stalk to one of the open windows, looking like a Roman emperor in a flowing toga.

"Hey," yelled Brewster out the window. "You lazy, blind, sons-a-bitches down there?"

"We're here, Mr. Harwick," answered a man's voice in the distance.

"You all right, sir?" said another.

"Wake up, you worthless bastards!"

Brewster moved towards Jim, scowling.

"Don't be too hard on them," said Jim. "It's better for everyone concerned if I'm not seen."

"Give me my watch," said Brewster, holding out his hand.

"Of course, sir. I was just admiring its workmanship."

After Jim handed over the watch, Brewster went to the bed, sat down, and opened the drawer of the night table. He looked at the stacks of neatly bound hundred dollar bills then at Jim.

"It's all there, sir," said Jim, smiling.

Brewster motioned to the telephone. "You hear that conversation?"

"Yes, I did."

"The superintendent of mine seven called Addison Chase a few minutes ago. Reported a fire. Company store and community hall burned clear to the ground. Too bad the houses didn't burn—along with the occupants."

"Destruction is always more exciting than victory, isn't it?" said Jim, getting up and walking around to the front of the desk. He sat on the front edge, crossing his legs.

Brewster watched him a moment. "You had the pluck to do that?"

"I put my two best men on it. You wanted to get things moving—now they're moving."

Brewster grinned. "I like your evil ways, Gentleman Jim."

Jim shook his head in disagreement. "It's the world that's evil. I'm just trying to get along in it."

Brewster laughed, and lit one of his thick black cigars. Jim glanced to the open windows, and could see the gray light of dawn appearing.

"I'm going to have to get back soon."

"Then why did you come?" asked Brewster, reclining against the large headboard of his bed.

"Business," replied Jim. "One pot's been stirred. Now we need to do the other."

Brewster blew a long stream of blue cigar smoke into the air. "You are an evil bastard. But I still like you. That fire was good. I can blame it on the miners. They start destroying company property it's just another nail in their coffin. I've been against calling in the National Guard, but this could be the excuse to do it. The Governor couldn't very well refuse. And the miners would be on their way out."

"I'm not so sure this is the right time for that," said Jim. "You see, you would still have the Breakers to contend with. Even if the Guard comes in, how long will the Breakers be here? How long before they leave without causing more trouble?"

"And causing me to spend more money keeping their worthless asses in camp," said Brewster.

"If you can't afford the price of war, you shouldn't start one, is my motto."

"Fine, fine," said Brewster, irritated at being lectured to. "What's in that mind of yours? What's this other pot that has to be stirred?"

Jim got up and began circling the desk, moving in and out of the lamp light like a specter, hands clasped confidently behind his back. "Right now," he began, "I'm sure the miners would love to retaliate against the Breakers for the fire. Maybe they will, but I very much doubt it. So we have to get the Breakers to *think* the miners have done something to them in retaliation."

"Like what?" asked Brewster.

"I haven't fully settled on that. But it'll cost money, I'm afraid."

"How much?"

A bit more than last time."

"I had a feeling that's where you were headed. Is this pot stirring going to produce any results?"

Jim seated himself on the front edge of the desk again. "Life's a treacherous game, Mr. Harwick. It all comes down to what you can get away with. But anything can be made to order. Even success."

Brewster clamped his thick cigar in the corner of his mouth, reached into the drawer of the night table, then tossed two packets of bound hundred dollar bills in Jim's direction.

Jim nodded his head politely. "Must be comforting to sleep beside a drawer full of money every night."

"It's for emergencies."

"Yes," said Jim, picking up the money from the floor and putting it in his pocket, "life's always full of little emergencies."

"You know, Gentleman Jim, I'm getting excited about this."

"Really?"

"Excited to see what you're going to do next."

Jim leaned against the desk and thought for a second. "Strange. Why is it we're more excited when doing evil, than when doing good?"

Brewster laughed loudly. "You sure are something. Just who the hell are you?"

Jim shrugged. "An outcast. An observer of the dreges of society."

"Well, for two thousand dollars I expect you to do more than observe."

"Your money has been very well spent, sir."

"Those miners brought this on themselves. And on their women and kids. It's not my fault, it's theirs."

"Yes. Ruthless people deserve ruthless justice," said Jim, and glanced to the windows. The horizon was growing brighter. "I'm afraid I have to go now."

———————

The Breakers' camp was just beginning to come to life. Smouldering fires from the night before were forced back to flames with the kindling of half-green sticks. Voices—tired and drunken and threatening—began to fill the air. Smoke from the rising fires quickly fogged everything with a thin haze. A fight broke out between two men, and a mob gathered, shouting encouragement. Other groups of men stood staring towards the housing area of mine seven. Long tails of smoke still drifted high in the air from the burnt remains of the company store and community hall.

"I hope they don't burn themselves out too soon," said a loud, raucous voice, "I still need to fill my pockets with more money."

A chorus of laughter greeted the man's words.

"Let's eat," shouted another voice.

The gang of Breakers began making their way in the direction of the large cooking fires, and boiling kettles of food and coffee, tended by sweating, spitting, grimy-looking cooks.

Meanwhile, Oracle remained sitting cross-legged in front of the tent he shared with Jim and Handsome. He tossed a handful of kindling onto the small fire in front of him then peeked apprehensively through the bushes. The Breakers' camp was now swarming with hundreds of hungry, rowdy men. Oracle kept low to the ground, watching, ready to scurry away and hide if any strangers came near. Then he saw Jim coming through the smoke and dust, and crowds of men, and sprang to his feet. His face was bright and alive now, and he swayed from side to side, excited and relieved at not being alone any more.

"Jim," he said happily, "I...I thought something bad happened to you. I...I was scared, Jim."

"Calm down," said Jim, patting Oracle on the head. "Everything's all right. I had to go talk to a man."

Jim sat on the ground, giving a sigh of relief, and pulled off his battered shoes and paper-thin socks. He began massaging his dirty feet. Oracle sat close to him, smiling.

"That walk seems to be getting longer," said Jim. "But it's profitable. Where's Handsome got to?"

Oracle frowned and stared down. "He sent me back alone after those fires started. I almost got lost, Jim. I started to cry."

"He sent you back alone? Why?"

"He...he said he had a sweet thing to see. A...a little jewel with hair like silk."

Jim stopped massaging his feet, and his expression became hard and dark. He looked in the direction of mine seven. "That won't do at all. It's not part of the plan. He could get caught."

"You want I should go find him, Jim?"

"No, no. You stay with me."

"Me and Handsome did good, huh, Jim?" asked Oracle, nodding in anticipation.

"You did admirable."

"An admirable fire," said Oracle, pleased with what he had done, and with winning Jim's praise. "The flames…the flames got as high as the tree tops."

Oracle continued to tell about the fire, but Jim wasn't listening, his eyes were still on mine seven. "This isn't good," he said to himself. "Not good at all. We have to stick to the plan or the wheels will come off."

"What's wrong, Jim? Did Handsome do something bad?"

"I don't know yet."

"But he was happy. He had a big smile when he talked about his jewel."

Jim turned to Oracle. His eyes had a menacing glare to them. "Better to cut your eyes out than look at a woman who will make you do crazy things—betray your friends."

"But I need my eyes, Jim."

"And so does Handsome. He may be suffering from a softening of the brain."

"Or the heart."

Jim couldn't help smiling, but his expression became hard again. "I hope Handsome isn't failing us."

"Life's a puzzle, I think," said Oracle, feeling Jim's uneasiness.

"A great puzzle," replied Jim. "But don't you love the adventure of it? Look." Jim pulled the two packets of hundred dollars bills from his coat pocket.

Oracle gave a surprised gasp. "Just like last time."

"More than last time. And we'll divide it evenly, like last time."

"You…you better keep mine for me. I always lose things."

"Most men have to sweat and claw their lives away for money like this, but we made it in one swoop. Crime may be a vicious thing, but it's all we've got to depend on."

"The man who gave you that must be good."

"I'm afraid not."

"Oh. I'll say a prayer for him then."

"Yes, he's going to need it. He has a very small soul."

"I'm hungry, Jim."

"You haven't filled your gullet, boy?"

"I was waiting for you and Handsome."

"Go, go. Take your plate and cup and load up."

"What about you, Jim?"

"I need to rest a bit. You go on."

Oracle crawled into the tent, grabbed his tin plate and cup, and spoon, and crawled quickly out the other side. He began running in the direction of one of the camp kitchens.

Jim got to his feet with a tired moan, walked a few yards in the direction of mine seven and stopped. "Don't let me down, Handsome," he said softly. "Don't become emotional, boy."

CHAPTER 10

"I'm so glad you changed your mind and came for lunch," said Isabel, escorting Abigail Harwick across the large entrance hall and out the tall French doors, and onto the immense slate-covered terrace.

Both women were wearing flowing summer dresses—Abigail's a deep pink as were her shoes and large sun hat that set off her vibrant red hair and pale green eyes. Isabel's dress was sky-blue as well as her shoes. The long sleeves of the dress flowed out behind her in the gentle afternoon breeze, giving her the façade of an imposing queen.

"Let's sit a while," said Isabel, motioning to a large round table and two chairs, "lunch isn't quite ready."

When the two were seated, Isabel removed a white linen napkin draping a decanter of brandy, bowl of ice, and two crystal glasses.

"Thank God," said Abigail when she saw the decanter. "I was afraid you were going to serve lemonade."

"Well, there's nothing wrong with us girls having a drop or two, every now and then."

"Yes. It helps take away the pain."

Isabel added an ice cube to each glass and poured the brandy. "Did you want a little water in it?"

"No, don't spoil it."

"Yes," said Isabel, handing a glass to Abigail, "things can get spoiled easily, can't they? Cheers."

The women touched glasses and took a delicate sip.

"We've known each other a long time now," began Isabel, "so I feel I can be honest with you."

"About what?"

"You. You're not the same person any more. It saddens me. I can see it in your eyes."

"See what?"

"Delusion, anger, resentment. And regret."

"Really?" said Abigail, sipping her drink. "I didn't think my eyes were that big."

Isabel smiled faintly. "I certainly wish you lived here year round."

"God forbid," said Abigail with obvious disgust. "Not that I don't love your company, Isabel, but this living in the wilderness thing isn't what I dream of."

"It does take getting use to. Not that much to do here, is there?"

"There's nothing to do here. No theaters, no restaurants, no country club, no parties. God, sometimes I wake up in the middle of the night ready to scream."

"Brewster seems to enjoy it though," said Isabel, adding a touch more brandy to their glasses.

"All he does is hunt and fish, and shout orders at everyone. Addison included."

"I know. Brewster's quite the he-man."

"I always wonder, if when he goes fishing, he stands along the river bank and commands the trout to jump onto his hook?"

Isabel and Abigail began laughing, began relaxing with one another. They each took a long sip of brandy.

"Thank you for calling. I needed to do something. Needed to get away," said Abigail.

"I'm sure it's not easy living with someone as demanding as Brewster," said Isabel, cautiously.

"Easy? Try the word, hell."

"I think that's the brandy talking," smiled Isabel.

"He's had affairs," said Abigail bitterly. "Two that I know of."

"Are you sure?"

"Without a doubt."

"I don't know what to say. That must have hurt you very deeply."

"At first, then when you realize you can't do anything about it, can't stop it, you make the decision not to care. That helps a lot."

"Perhaps. But if things like that go on, why do you stay?"

"Why do you live on an estate like this? Ride in a chauffeured automobile?"

"Very well put," said Isabel, extending her glass, and she and Abigail clinked glasses and took another long sip.

"You have your own money, surely," continued Isabel. "You don't have to answer to anyone. You're free as a bird."

"Free as Brewster let's me be."

"I think you're wrong, there."

Abigail saw a certain look in Isabel's eyes, and set her drink down. "I don't understand what you're saying."

"You said, this life here isn't what you dream of. Then what do you dream of?"

"Lots of things. And why would you think I'm free as a bird?"

Isabel set her drink down, leaned in towards Abigail, and spoke softly. "But you are, my dear."

"I don't understand."

"All that property."

"What property?"

"You had to have seen the papers; had to have signed them."

Abigail thought a moment. "Yes, there were certain papers Brewster had me sign; months after we were married, but I paid no attention."

"Naughty girl."

"Brewster said it was just banking arrangement things, I…"

"It was quite a bit more than that," said Isabel, picking up her glass and taking a sip.

"Like what?"

"You, my naive girl, own half of Harwick Coal Company. Along with several large lumber mills in Pennsylvania and Michigan. You've been sitting on the proverbial gold mine."

"You must be wrong."

"Addison has shown me the papers. He can show them to you. If you're interested."

Abigail stared at Isabel then took a long swallow of her drink.

"You're worth millions, dear Abigail," said Isabel. "You've been free all along, only Brewster didn't want you to know it, unless he had too. He never had any respect for you then—or now."

Abigail took another long swallow of her brandy, got up, and walked slowly to the far side of the terrace. There was confusion and disbelief on her face. Isabel came up behind her and put an arm around her.

"Don't you think it's time to live life the way you want?" said Isabel calmly. "Why be led around on a leash like one of Brewster's hunting dogs?"

"Is Addison sure of this?"

"He's positive, and so am I. You have your own empire. All you have to do is take it."

"How?" asked Abigail, turning to Isabel. "Brewster won't..."

"Addison will handle everything for you. Give him Power of Attorney and he will deal with Brewster. You won't be alone in this. Langdon Hallgren is very interested in helping also."

"I think I met him once at a dinner party; Chicago or New York, I think."

"He remembers you. And was impressed with you."

"But why help me?"

"As a favor to Addison. Langdon controls many people in Washington, and all over this state. He claps his hands and they jump."

"I...I don't know...I," began Abigail, then took a few steps away, giving herself time to think.

"Don't hesitate, Abigail, don't be afraid of Brewster," said Isabel, coming up behind her. "You need to decide quickly. If not for yourself, then for you daughters."

Abigail turned. "My children?"

"Do this for them. I've heard from Addison how Brewster treats them."

"Yes," said Abigail softly. "Like strangers; like they just walked in off the street; like they don't belong to him."

"Brewster's the one who doesn't belong," said Isabel, putting an arm around Abigail again. "It's time for you to begin a new life. A life you deserve."

A round yellow moon was beginning to show itself from behind the ragged high ridges north of the Breakers' camp. Campfires burned in every direction as the carousing men played cards and rolled dice. The usual fist fights and knife fights broke out here and there, but they had become so common no one paid much attention any more.

Over near the railroad cars, Hildscheimer and his all-girl orchestra had set up their chairs and music stands, and the evening concert was underway. Row upon row of squatting, and sitting, men surrounded the orchestra. Grinning hungrily, and with eyes bleary from too much whiskey, the mob stared with anticipation at what might lay ahead in the late, dark hours—if they had enough money. The ladies stood out boldly in the light of the kerosene lamps; their yellow dresses almost glowing as they played one out-of-key tune after the other. The violins, banjos, trombones, and a cello, sounded more in competition with one another than in harmony. Hildscheimer waved his baton, but couldn't quite get in rhythm either.

A few shots rang out on the east side of the camp, but were ignored; as were the camp guards when they began beating the trigger-happy miscreant with their rifle butts, and dragged him off by his heels.

Secure in their own private little sanctuary, Gentleman Jim, Handsome, and Oracle sat silently at their campfire finishing their evening meal; spoons scraping against the tin plates. Jim kept throwing sidelong glances at Handsome—wondering glances. Oracle finished licking his plate clean then watched Jim. He could feel his uneasiness and tension. Handsome ate rapidly and wiped his plate with a chunk of biscuit. He chewed it greedily as if he hadn't eaten for days. He gave a gratified sigh, stretched out on the ground, and gave a loud belch.

Jim seemed like a lump of stone, sitting there, staring at nothing. Oracle became more agitated by Jim's silence. He tried to think of something to say to drive away the gnawing foreboding growing inside him.

"Jim," Oracle finally said, almost in a whisper, "this place has become poisonous with people. I think we should go away."

Jim smiled faintly, and looked towards the chaos of the main camp. "Not quiet yet. We've important things to do."

"The Devil is down there, Jim," said Oracle.

Handsome laughed and sat up, slapping Oracle repeatedly on his large shoulders. "It's amazing the things you come up with."

Oracle started to smile, but stopped and placed a hand gently on Handsome's arm. "You need to be careful, Handsome."

"I'm always careful. But I'm still hungry, I need more. So do you, Oracle."

"No," replied Oracle, shaking his head, frowning, "not right now, I…"

"Go, Oracle," said Jim. "That little pile of mess you just had won't half fill that belly of yours."

Oracle simply looked down and shook his head again.

"Then get Handsome some, before he starves to death," said Jim, waving his hand to get Oracle moving. "Fill his plate, make him burst."

Jim and Handsome laughed, causing Oracle to finally smile broadly. He grabbed Handsome's plate and cup and hurried away.

Handsome watched Oracle disappear into the smoky darkness, saying, "He's right about that bunch. We may be living out here in the open, but it feels like we're in a sewer with large, stinking rats."

"That's because we are," said Jim, setting his plate down. "This is all too much, too big, for their tiny brains. Let them drink themselves blind and maim each other. It's the man who takes the risks that makes things move, not money-grubbers like them."

"How much longer we going to stay?" asked Handsome.

Jim shrugged. "We're going to have to show a bit more grit. The money-well hasn't gone dry yet."

Jim got to his feet and moved to the edge of the nearby trees. He stared towards mine seven. Dim lights could be seen scattered among the houses and the mine itself. Tiny dark figures of men could be seen every so often, passing before the glow of the bare light bulbs. The entire area was alive with armed miners.

"They're certainly stirred up since the fire," said Jim. "Moving around like a swarm of ants."

"Ants are easy to step on," said Handsome, walking up beside Jim.

"I need you to take another stroll," said Jim.

"Where?"

"Up there, to the mine. Think you can do it? It won't be as easy as before."

Handsome smiled, unafraid. "I'll be as quiet as a shadow."

"Find the powder bunker," said Jim. "Bring back six or eight sticks of dynamite—and fuses and blasting caps."

"You always have things rolling around in your mind, don't you?"

"The night holds promise for people like us. And it brings us money."

"The gospel of gold," said Handsome.

Jim turned to Handsome, but his eyes still held an unfriendly gaze. "Go carefully, I need you to come back safely."

"The bullet hasn't been made that can kill me," said Handsome confidently.

Handsome started away, but Jim put a hand on his shoulder, stopping him. "I wet-nurse Oracle because he's such a pleasure to me. But I can't wet-nurse you."

Handsome looked at Jim, puzzled. "Meaning?"

"The night of the fire. You sent Oracle back alone. For some reason he thought you had a girl to see. A piece of fluff."

Handsome grinned. "She's a looker, Jim. You should…"

"Now's not the time for that," Jim interrupted coldly.

"When the hell is? We can't let life pass us by, can we? Or a great woman."

"I'm sure she's as pure as a drop of holy water, but…"

"Hopefully she's got some hell in her, too," said Handsome with that captivating smile of his. "Or things will get boring real quick," he added with a wink. "I look at her like she's a gift to me. Doesn't it say somewhere in the Bible, a good woman is God's gift to man—something like that?"

"And after Adam, her second companion was the Devil," replied Jim dryly.

Handsome laughed and walked away. "I'll be back before daylight."

Jim watched till Handsome faded into the darkness, then crossed back to the tiny campfire and stood looking at it. Oracle came hurrying up, carrying Handsome's tin plate heavy with food, and his tin cup, slopping over with hot coffee. He glanced around with searching eyes.

"Where…where'd he go?"

"You're disappointed, aren't you?" said Jim.

"I came as fast as I could, Jim."

"I'm disappointed too, Oracle. I think Handsome is letting us down."

The moon was high and bright when Handsome led Naomi by the hand into a thicket of scrub brush and a tangle of blackberry bushes.

"Hold on," whispered Naomi, "I got my dress caught."

Handsome quickly unhooked the hem of her dress from the sharp thorns of a berry bush, and gave her silky, long legs a slow stroke with his fingers. Naomi slapped them away.

"Settle down, boy," she said. "I didn't come out here to let you get frisky then run off."

Handsome smiled and rubbed his nose against hers, saying, "Then why'd you come?"

"You said you needed to talk about something important."

"Well, I do."

"You keep sneakin' around my house at night somebody's goin' to start shootin' at you."

"You'd be worth every shot."

Naomi smiled. "Really?"

The glow of the moonlight revealed their young eager faces to one another; their eyes shining with desire.

"Well," said Naomi, "what you got to say?"

"It's time for you and me to leave this place."

"And where we supposed to be goin' to?" asked Naomi, her eyebrows raised in skepticism.

"Anywhere your beautiful little heart desires, sweetheart."

"Just walk on down that long dusty road, wavin' goodbye to everybody, huh?"

"Just till we're clear of here."

"Then what, whisper a bunch of honey-coated words in my ear? Words that don't mean nothin'?"

Handsome reached into his coat pocket and brought out a roll of hundred dollar bills wrapped tightly with a dirty piece of string. Naomi let out a gasp.

"That real?" Naomi asked, reaching for the money.

Handsome pulled the roll back out of reach. "Don't get any more real than this."

"I knew right from the start you wasn't any coal miner."

"How come you're always wanting me to be a coal miner? Those poor bindle-stiffs are born broke, and they die broke. That what you want? Live here, scratching, clawing, and starving, till you wrinkle up and fall over?"

"No, I don't want that. I'd rather die right now. I'm tired of the sickening stink of the coal dust, and the dirt that's always on you; on what you eat, what you wear. You can taste it in your mouth and nose, mornin', noon, and night."

"This is what'll take that taste away," said Handsome, holding up the roll of money. "And I got more—hid out where I can get it easy. These little green pieces of paper are a new home, new car, new clothes; a new life."

Naomi studied Handsome's face then took a step back. "How do I know you ain't lyin'?"

Handsome took her hand and pressed her fingers tightly around the roll of money. "This is yours. You hang on to it till I get back."

"Why can't we go now? Why wait?"

"Cause it ain't that simple just yet. You can't go running off wearing that skimpy dress and no shoes."

"The hell I can't."

"And I got something to do first, then I"ll be back."

"When?"

"If not tomorrow night, then the next night for sure. You be ready. Hat, coat, shoes, and a blanket. Once we're away from here, we'll hop a train or maybe buy a car. Then we're on our way to anywhere we want. And we don't look back; not for nothing or nobody."

"I never want to see this place, or hear about it, ever again."

"You be ready," said Handsome, grabbing her and kissing her hard and long.

Naomi clutched his hair and cap with both hands and kissed him back just as hard. Handsome's hand went up under her dress and began stroking the inside of her thigh. She shoved him away with all her strength, and he fell backwards to the ground.

"You want this back," said Naomi, shaking the roll of money at him, "and a little something else, you better do what you say, sweet-talker."

Naomi leaped over Handsome like a wild deer and ran out of the moonlight. Handsome lay there, grinning, and watching her run. "You sure are going to be a handful," he said softly.

―――――――――

The round yellow moon disappeared in a flood of thick, dark storm clouds, swept in by a swift, rising wind; bringing with it a chilling air and the scent of rain. The sound of thunder rolled in closer to the Breakers' camp, and the wind scattered the red coals of the campfires first one way then another. The men began retreating to their tents or inside the long line of boxcars. Tiny droplets of rain began tapping against the tents, and the fires began hissing and popping, and fading into clouds of smoke.

Gentleman Jim, Handsome, and Oracle moved in a line, close together, without a sound. The scouring wind drowned out their footsteps on the gravel of the railroad bed near the string of boxcars. Jim stepped into the darkness between two of the cars, Handsome and Oracle beside him. They all waited as men stood at the open doors of the far cars; some spitting tobacco juice, some puking from too much whiskey, but most were just urinating.

Jim spoke quietly. "Your clever feats always impress me, Handsome. You got there and back in no time, with exactly what was needed."

"It wasn't that hard," replied Handsome. "There was a sign, big as a barn door, at the far end of the mine buildings that said, 'Powder Bunker. Keep Away'. Picking the lock didn't take long."

"You're more valuable than my right arm," said Jim.

"Are you sure this is right, Jim?" asked Oracle.

"I already told you, we're simply eliminating obstacles. Not people."

"Obstacles," repeated Oracle, thinking about the word.

"Obstacles into stepping stones," continued Jim.

"More like tombstones," said Handsome.

The rain began to hammer down in big, cold, smacking drops, hitting hard against everything. Jim, Handsome, and Oracle, pulled their caps down tight on their heads, and turned up the flimsy collars of their coats.

"Protect the fuses," said Jim frantically, "and your matches."

All three pulled their coats snuggly to themselves. Underneath each coat were three sticks of dynamite, tied together with twine. A blasting cap and long fuse were attached to the sticks.

Jim turned to Oracle. "You remember what I told you? You remember exactly what to do?"

"Just like you showed me, Jim. I wouldn't forget."

Jim stooped low and hurried along the boxcars with Handsome and Oracle following, the heavy rain splattering against their hunched forms. Silently, Jim disappeared under one of the cars; Handsome went under a second, and Oracle a third. Each man set his three sticks of dynamite on the long steel rods running underneath the floor boards of the cars. Carefully they took a match from their shirt pockets, scratched it against one of the rods. The matches hissed to life and the fuses were lit.

A long, jagged flash of lightning split the darkness as Jim came out from under his car and rushed back in the direction he had come from. Thunder suddenly rumbled in shaking the ground, and Handsome rolled out from under his car and fell in behind Jim. Oracle appeared next and scurried after them. When they reached the end of the line of boxcars, Jim stopped, knelt down, and looked back. Handsome and Oracle were close beside him. They waited for the explosions. A full minute passed before Jim got to his feet, frowning and worried.

"The fuses are no good," whispered Jim savagely.

"They could be slow burners," said Handsome.

"You want me to go look, Jim?" asked Oracle.

"No," snapped Jim.

"I'm sorry, Jim," replied Oracle, like a child who was about to be punished.

"Nothing to be sorry about," said Jim calmly. "Sometimes things don't go according to plan."

Curious, Jim began walking slowly back along the boxcars. He was stooping low again, hoping to see if there were any sparks from the fuses. The pounding rain made it hard to see. Oracle was right behind Jim, but Handsome held back a few yards, not convinced that the fuses were no good.

"Jim?" said Oracle quietly.

"What?" answered Jim, still moving slowly forward.

"Maybe we'll have to find some other stepping stones."

"I'm beginning to think you're…"

The three box cars were ripped apart one after the other in a deafening roar of flame and smoke. Jim, Oracle, and Handsome were thrown to the ground. Their eyes filled with shock at the destruction spewing high into the air. Men could be heard screaming; calling for help; calling for their mothers—their fathers. Boards and flaming debris began dropping everywhere, along with bloody arms, legs, hands, heads, and torsos. Lightning streaked against the blue-black sky, and seconds later the drumming of thunder added to the confusion.

"Damn," said Handsome to himself, shaken by what he had seen.

"It's the pit of Hell," cried Oracle. "We're at the pit of Hell."

"Get up, get up," said Jim, struggling to his feet. "Do exactly as I do."

Jim began running to the center of the camp; Handsome and Oracle right behind. The tent city was alive with running, shouting, cursing men. The women of the all-girl orchestra, whose tents were near the line of boxcars, were running in every direction, screaming and crying, and falling in the mud with only blankets wrapped around them.

Jim charged into the swirl of confusion and yelling, shouting: "The miners! It's the miners!"

Handsome and Oracle began shouting the same thing as loud as they could. Jim motioned frantically in one direction, while Handsome and Oracle motioned in a different direction.

"I saw them," shouted Jim. "I saw them!"

A hand grasped Jim's coat collar and jerked him completely around. "Where are they?" shouted Garlow, dressed only in wet, dirty pants, and barefooted.

"That way, Mr. Garlow," replied Jim. "They ran that way, towards the mine."

"There's bodies all over hell's half acre," roared Bully Boy as he ran up, dressed in thin, filthy long johns.

"It's horrible," cried Jim, "horrible." He covered his face with his hands.

Handsome continued pointing towards mine seven, shouting, "Up there. They went up there!"

Oracle began patting Jim gently on the back, to console him in his grief, and the rain streamed down mercilessly.

CHAPTER 11

By morning, the late night deluge had passed on. The sky was clear, and the sun beat down white and hot. But Addison Chase's office was cool. The windows were all open and the ceiling fan revolved slowly with a whisper of air. Addison sat at his desk, dressed impeccably as usual. Hugh Underhill, Governor Hallgren's aide, dressed as richly and impressively as Addison, paced back and forth in front of the desk. Addison watched him patiently.

Finally Underhill spoke. "I couldn't have planned it any better myself." He turned to Addison. "You're positive Sheriff Deets knows what he's talking about?"

"He went out there," replied Addison. "Saw it. The Breakers' camp is a mess. They're still picking up pieces of people everywhere."

"This couldn't have happened at a better time," said Underhill, resuming his pacing. "Once the governor announces this to the newspapers, he'll have the perfect excuse to send in the National Guard. It's for the public's safety."

"And it let's me off the hook," said Addison.

"Absolutely. Now you don't have to request the National Guard be brought in to settle this strike. And Harwick will have no idea you're involved in this in any way—until it's too late."

Underhill slapped his hands together and clasped them tightly, as if praying to some personal god. There was a knock on the office door.

"In," said Addison loudly.

The door opened and Jeffers, the head clerk, appeared. "Mr. Addison, your mother and Mrs. Harwick just arrived."

"In please," said Addison, getting up.

Jeffers opened the door wide, smiling and bowing. "Mrs. Chase, please," he said extending his hand into the room. "And so nice to have met you, Mrs. Harwick."

The two women smiled and nodded as they walked boldly in, and Jeffers left quickly, closing the door.

"Ladies, please," said Addison, motioning to two chairs near his desk. He held one of them for his mother, and Underhill held the other for Abigail.

"Mrs. Harwick," began Underhill, with an engaging smile, "it's an extreme pleasure to meet you."

"Thank you, Mr. Underhill. Isabel tells me you made a special trip all the way from the state capitol."

"An enjoyable change of pace for me. And I'm sure this is going to be an enjoyable first meeting. One of many I hope."

Underhill leaned against the desk, and confidently crossed his arms. He and Abigail eyed each other up and down with approval.

"You're awfully young to be a governor's aide, aren't you?" asked Abigail, still surveying Underhill's tall, lean body, and strong, handsome face.

"My father always said I was born to be in politics. He was right, it's in my blood. Along with the determination to become very rich."

"Nothing wrong with that," said Isabel.

Underhill nodded to her then turned his attention to Abigail. "And what about you, Mrs. Harwick? You don't have anything against becoming very, very rich do you?"

"Now you're flirting with me, Mr. Underhill."

Underhill gave a short laugh. "Intelligent as well as beautiful. I like that."

"But I thought I was rich already."

"What we're here to discuss," said Underhill, "you and I, Addison, and Isabel, goes far beyond what most people think the word rich means."

"Tell me more," said Abigail.

Underhill looked to Addison, saying, "If you'll allow me?"

"Please," replied Addison. "That's why you're here."

Underhill began pacing around the room, rubbing his chin with his long, thin fingers, collecting his thoughts then he began. "Isabel has already informed you of your position with Harwick Coal. A very dominating position to say the least. You have the opportunity and ability to control a vast wealth; an empire. But we have to do this all quickly; like a razor cut—and deeply. Not hesitating for one second, not looking back for one second."

"Abigail has agreed to sign the papers giving me Power of Attorney," said Addison. "We just have to decide on a new name for Abigail's empire."

"And the lumber mills," added Isabel. "I think there's quite a lot of money to be made there also. Let's not scoff at that."

"I agree," said Underhill, coming back to the front of Addison's desk and seating himself on the edge. "You're about to become a legend, Mrs. Harwick."

Abigail smiled slightly, and Isabel reached over, placing a reassuring hand on Abigail's arm.

"This all sounds very intriguing," said Abigail, "but how is all this going to happen?"

"Beginning right at this moment," replied Underhill, "you have very powerful people ready to set you on a golden throne."

"Who else besides the people in this room?" asked Abigail.

"Governor Hallgren as I said. As for the rest, there are certain senators and congressmen in Washington, and the state capitol, who will all come into play later. They're all firm friends of the governor. But most important are the gentlemen of the railroad cartel." Underhill turned to Addison. "We've already talked with them. They know about the Colossal vein, and have been shown the geologist's report and map."

"Then they should have no doubts," said Addison.

"And you think you can take all this away from Brewster?" asked Abigail.

"It belongs to you," said Addison. "Not Brewster."

"Have you explained that to Brewster?" said Abigail, cynically, still not convinced of the plan that was being presented.

"This first meeting is only the beginning," said Underhill. "There will have to be many more. But our friends at the railroad will deal the opening blow."

"How?" asked Abigail.

"The freight tolls to move Harwick Coal will go up substantially, very substantially, but the coal from your mines will be given special preference."

"Plus," said Addison, "certain large coal brokers in New York, Chicago, and Philadelphia, will inform Brewster that their storage yards and shipping wharves are filled to capacity, making the major distribution centers no longer available to him. If Brewster can't get his coal to market, there's no point in mining it. And there will be no money coming in."

"There's much more that will be done, Abigail," said Isabel, "but that's entirely up to you."

"Brewster is at the edge of the abyss," said Addison. "All he needs is a push."

Abigail's eyes moved from Addison to Underhill, to Isabel, and back to Addison. She stood up. Addison and the others watched apprehensively.

"Well," said Abigail finally, "what are you waiting for? Start pushing."

Addison and Underhill sprang to their feet, all smiles. Isabel rose from her chair, her eyes on Addison, as if to tell him she had no doubt that Abigail would come over to them as she had predicted.

"Thank you, Abigail," said Addison. "I won't let you down."

"None of us will," added Underhill.

"But I'd like to hear more about Governor Hallgren's part in this," said Abigail. "And more about the railroad people."

"I'm at your complete disposal," said Underhill.

"Then lunch this afternoon?" said Abigail. "The Palmyra Hotel?"

"Perfect," said Underhill, "that's where I'm staying. Shall we say eleven-thirty?"

"Fine."

Abigail started for the office door with Isabel beside her. Addison rushed past them to open the door.

"Allow me to walk you ladies to your car," he said.

"Thank you, Addison," said Abigail with a slight nod; a nod a queen would give to one of her lackeys. She was beginning to feel, and believe, she *was* the possessor of an empire.

"Addison, one moment, please," said Underhill.

Abigail and Isabel continued on out, and Addison closed the door halfway.

Underhill walked up, saying, "The Governor is waiting for my call. I'm going to tell him to begin; start the machine."

"I agree."

"There won't be any turning back now. Not for anything or anyone."

"Why should there be?"

Underhill patted Addison on the shoulder. "We're going to work well together. And, I wouldn't mind working more closely with Abigail. God, what a beauty." Underhill looked out the door to where Abigail and Isabel stood talking, waiting for Addison.

"Hugh," said Addison after a few seconds.

"Yes?"

"Don't forget to call the Governor."

Underhill gave an embarrassed grin and walked back towards the desk. "Hold on to your hat, here we go," he said loudly, and began dialing the telephone.

Addison went on out, put an arm around Isabel and his other around Abigail, and escorted them from the outer office. All three were smiling, and whispering excitedly to one another.

The Breakers' camp was still in turmoil, and the hot sun, beginning to dry the trampled, muddy ground, was causing it to steam, making the entire camp appear like a misty swamp. Large gangs of men, with picks and shovels, were digging graves through the sticky mud and into hard, dry soil. They were shirtless, and sweat was pouring from them. They dug and cursed, and blew snot from their noses to clear away the stink of the coal dust now drifting down from the mine.

Other gangs of men were approaching the waiting graves with blankets or burlap bags containing bodies, or parts of bodies. Far behind them were the railroad tracks and the three blackened and burned out boxcars. The walls had all collapsed, but most of the flooring and steel wheels were there. Every now and then a whiff of smoke would drift up from the charred remains of wood and flesh.

There was no thought or talk of the noonday meal; tin cups were repeatedly filled with whiskey, and the drinkers' hate-filled talk turned to revenge and killing.

Otis Garlow, a belt of ammunition around his waist, a pistol tucked in his back pocket, and a rifle in his right hand, came stomping through the slick, gray mud. "Bully Boy," he bellowed. "Bully Boy, where are you?"

"Here!" he answered, and came slipping and sliding through the mud. He, too, had a belt of ammunition around his waist, and two large revolvers jambed behind the belt.

Suddenly rifle fire erupted. Ten, twenty, forty rifles; then fifty, then a hundred. Lines of men stood at the edge of the camp shooting in the direction of mine seven's housing area.

"What the hell they think they're doing?" yelled Garlow.

"They're on the prod," replied Bully Boy. "Let 'em go."

"They can't hit a damn thing from here," snapped Garlow.

"They got to get it out of their system," said Bully Boy.

"Don't worry, I'll get it out of their system," said Garlow.

"Otis, Otis," said Hildsheimer, scurrying up to them, his shoes and trouser cuffs caked with mud.

"What the hell you want?" growled Garlow.

"Mein little daffodils; they're terrified," said Hildsheimer. "They want to go. What am I to do?"

"Tell those overpaid sluts to stay right where they are," replied Garlow.

"But they don't want to get blowed up. Poof."

"And how tough will it be to replace them if they do?" asked Garlow.

Hildsheimer shrugged. "Two, three days, maybe, but..."

Garlow grabbed Hildsheimer by his shirt collar and pulled him close. "Listen, you little German weasel, I just had over seventy men blown to kingdom come, and I'm not concerned about you and your trash bitches."

"Then I'm afraid we'll have to raise our prices," said Hildscheimer with a helpless gesture.

Garlow gave an animal-like roar and flung Hildsheimer away, sending him flat on his back into a deep pool of mud. The men, nearby, began laughing and pointing at him.

The rifle fire continued without pause, and other Breakers began joining in; even those with small pistols, that couldn't reach a hundred yards.

"Call all the camp bosses together," ordered Garlow to Bully Boy.

A wide grin came to Bully Boy's face. "We going to do something?"

"We're going to kill something."

Morgan McAlister and Tom Mitchell moved carefully along the junked together barricades that stretched from one end of the housing area to the other, and on past the burned out skeletons of the company store and community hall, then on up towards the mine. Clutching their rifles Morgan and Tom crouched behind an overturned coal wagon, looking towards the Breakers' camp. The gunfire had stopped more than an hour ago, but the camp was still alive with the dark figures of men constantly on the move.

"They'll be coming before long," said Mitchell.

Morgan nodded. "Is Pike and his men in position?"

"Should be by now," answered Mitchell, looking up towards the mine. "They're on the high ridge back of the mine. But the Breakers could still get around behind them."

"Pike will just have to stop them," said Morgan.

"The Breakers got plenty of ammunition, that's for sure. Or they wouldn't have been firing like they were."

Morgan turned and leaned against the coal wagon. He didn't look at Mitchell as he spoke. "How much ammunition you think we have?"

"Not much."

"And food?"

"Even less."

Morgan sat down on the ground, leaning his rifle against the coal wagon. He rubbed his sweaty hands together, and looked up at Mitchell.

"Booth came by late last night; said some of the miners had come to see him about ending this."

"What?" said Mitchell, shocked. He squatted beside Morgan. "The dirty bastards."

"Booth said he wouldn't do anything unless I agreed. Said he would call Chase and get the Breakers called off, if we go back to work."

"Not after all this, Morgan, no."

"Over half of us here are down to eating corn mush twice a day. How soon before that runs out?"

"Our hope hasn't run out," said Mitchell defiantly. "And we still have our rifles."

"We don't need rifles. We need work."

"Go back to the way we were?" said Mitchell, a troubled look on his face. "What about the men shot dead here? What about Zweig, burned alive in his own store?"

"What about those men down there," said Morgan, "blown up in those railroad cars?"

"The hell with that Breaker scum."

"Who blew them up? Why? It wasn't us."

"Maybe it was one of God's angels."

"More like one of the Devil's angels," replied Morgan. "We're not in control of anything any more. We're just desperate men now. Our women and children are starting to go hungry."

"I'd rather die at this barricade than let Chase and Harwick win; let them go on living like emperors on our sweat and misery."

"It isn't just you, it's our families too."

"What kind of future do they have if we lose?"

Morgan stared down a moment, then got up and wiped the sweat from his face. He grabbed his rifle and walked away. "Don't let me be afraid," he whispered. "God, don't let me be afraid."

Mitchell stood watching Morgan, suddenly feeling weak and unable to move. He, too, was beginning to feel the desperation he had seen in Morgan's eyes; the desperation that was seeping into all of them.

It was close to sunset when the Breakers began their approach. They were in scattered bunches, crouching low, but hurrying—hundreds of them; silent like ants. They came from all directions, completely surrounding the housing area and the mine.

The miners watched tensely as the hunched figures rushed towards them across the open fields, along the web of drainage ditches, disappearing momentarily behind the tall, brittle patches of scrub brush, and clumps of dead, leaning trees.

High up behind the mine, the Breakers there had found plenty of cover behind large boulders, in deep gullys, and the clusters of fallen, rotted tree trunks. As they began their advance, they stirred up the thick layers of coal dust all around them, and it rose quickly into the hot evening air in streaming curtains, and drifted down to where Kelly Pike and thirty other miners waited. They held their fire—not from bravery or cunning—but because their ammunition was dangerously low.

The hundreds of Breakers approaching the main barricades of the miners, down below, suddenly stopped moving. They kneeled, waited a moment, then began shooting. The gunfire blended into one horrific roar, along with the yells and curses of the men behind the guns. Most were drunk and unafraid, wanting to kill; wanting to see the ground soaked with miners' blood.

The miners' houses, automobiles and trucks took the brunt of the withering volleys that never ceased. Windshields were shattered, tires were shredded; fenders and doors were riddled with jagged holes. The outsides of the frail houses shook, as if someone were hammering on them. The thin board siding became splintered and gouged. There wasn't one window or door frame that wasn't riddled with holes. The dusty main street, and side alleys, spurted plumes of dust as bullets tore into the ground. Even the wooden sidewalks began to splinter. Dogs howled from their hiding places under the houses. Inside, women and children began to scream from the ricocheting bullets. Shattered pieces of cedar roof shingles spun through the air.

Growing careless and overconfident, the Breakers began to rush forward; their gunfire never abating. A wild cry rose from them as they charged.

"Fire," shouted Morgan. "Fire!"

The long, thin line of miners opened fire, and a wall of lead tore into the Breakers. Those who weren't hit, kept running and shooting and yelling, oblivious to the rows of dead and wounded piling up behind them. The screams of the wounded only made the charging men think victory was in their grasp.

Behind the miners' barricades, men began to fall and die; crying out in agony. Hundreds of bullets were ripping and whining all around them. Some men simply stared a moment at the bloody hole in their chest or stomach, surprised, then fell forward; others writhed in the dirt, turning it black with their blood; some cried, realizing death had come quickly and without remorse.

"Like hell with the lid off, ain't it?" shouted one grinning miner to the man next to him.

"We're all dead as Julius Caesar, this keeps up," replied the man, firing his bolt-action rifle as fast as he could.

"I need cartridges," yelled another man, holding out his hand to the miner to his right.

"You've come to the wrong place, boyo," the man yelled back. "I'm out! It's claws and fangs from here on!"

In less than a second, both men were flung backwards to the ground and never moved.

On the high ridge above the rear of the mine, Kelly Pike and his men had run out of ammunition, and were flinging sticks of dynamite; the fuses burning for only four or five seconds. The unending rows of Breakers kept coming. Then minutes later the unnerving shock of the dynamite blasts began to take its toll. The Breakers slowed their advance, then stopped completely. The boulders and rotted trees gave little protection now, and the Breakers began to panic and scramble back up the steep slopes. The screams of dying men and bloody body parts filled the air.

Back at the main barricades, the relentless, punishing gunfire on both sides began to dwindle; then just scattered pockets of rapid firing were heard here and there. The last rays of the sun vanished, and the growing darkness was the only thing that forced the battle to an end.

The miners were the first to stop shooting—most had only two or three cartridges left in their pockets. Up behind the mine, the dynamite blasts became sporadic. Bloody, and black with coal dust, Kelly Pike continued throwing one stick of dynamite after another, calling for his men to keep fighting. But half of them were dead; the other half wounded, and too dazed to fight.

The mass of Breakers that had come within eighty yards of the main barricades retreated into the welcome darkness. They began running, ignoring the wounded stumbling along ahead of them, jumping over the dead and wounded on the ground—ground slippery with pools of blood.

For a long time the miners remained motionless and exhausted; the black night hiding everything. Then they got slowly up, and began to count their losses. A low, unending moaning filled the air; the moaning of women for their dead and dying husbands, and brothers—for the dead and dying children lying in the riddled houses.

The Breakers were just as stunned and disoriented as the miners. Their bluster and savagery had deserted them in the reality of sudden death and butchery. No campfires were lighted. Some of the men sat huddled together talking softly; but most lay stretched out on the ground behind their tents, out of sight, incase the miners began shooting again. The cries of the wounded and dying Breakers far out in the darkness filtered through the camp, but they were ignored.

From under many of the miners' houses, the frightened, shivering dogs put up a mournful howling—a lament—sensing that death was still all around them.

"Morgan, you there?" asked the subdued voice of one of the miners.

Morgan came to the screen door of his dark house and looked out. Twelve fatigued, and disheveled, men stood in a tight group at the foot of the porch steps. Morgan came quietly out, then realized Tom Mitchell and Kelly Pike were in the group.

"We've taken some heavy loses, Morgan," began Mitchell, his voice tired and hoarse. "We need to talk."

"I know," Morgan answered softly.

"What's left of us are on guard, or at home with the wounded and dying," continued Mitchell. "But we speak for those men as well as ourselves."

"We've got to end this," said a man angrily.

"I've changed my mind, Morgan," said Mitchell, swallowing noticeably, "I think you need to have Booth tell Chase we'll do as he asks."

"No," said Pike loudly. "The Breakers are beaten. You saw how they ran."

"And we're just as beat as they are," said a man next to Pike.

"Worse," said another man. "We've got more women and children dead."

"We've got to keep on," pleaded Pike.

"Ah, quiet down, Kelly," said a man. "We ain't got nothin' to keep on with." He stepped forward and looked up at Morgan. "When I came to work as head carpenter here, I helped a lot of these men fix up their homes. Now I'm going to build coffins for them and their families."

"I know, Tully," replied Morgan. "I've already counted the dead."

"I don't want to build any more coffins," said Tully, and walked away.

Morgan came down the porch steps so he could get a close look at the men's faces in the dark. "So we end it then?" he asked.

"What Chase and Harwick do to us now don't make much difference," said a man quietly.

"Yes, it does," said Pike, a fierce look in his eyes.

"Kelly," said another man, "we're wore out. Mind, body, and soul. Can't you see that?"

"What do we have left to fight for?" asked another man.

"Your life, that's what," replied Pike.

"My life?" said the man. "I'd like to chew it up and spit it in God's face."

Before Pike could reply, the man turned and shuffled away, his heavy work boots scuffing through the powdery dust of the street. Another miner stepped up close, so Morgan could see the anger on his face.

"I say we sabotage the mine," began the man. "Blow up the pumps, the fans; let it all go back to hell where it belongs."

"No," said Morgan, and Mitchell, quickly.

"Don't act the fool, Sayer," added Mitchell.

The man gave an angry swept of his arm and walked away.

"Do the rest of you men feel the same?" asked Morgan.

"No," said a man. "There's lots of us feel like Kelly, here. That we shouldn't knuckle under. But we've paid a dear price already."

"I'm not knuckling under," said Pike. "I'll fight on alone if I have to."

"Quit talking crazy," shouted Mitchell. "You know you…"

"Go to hell, all of you," shouted Pike, and stalked off.

"Kelly," called Mitchell.

"Let him go," said Morgan. "How many of the men are for going on?"

"Don't really know," answered Mitchell. "But we'd better find out."

"Soon as it's daylight," said Morgan, "call everyone together."

"Nothing else we can do, Morgan," said Mitchell with a shrug.

Morgan walked back into his house, and Mitchell and the others went on up the street in silence.

From behind the darkness of the screen door, Morgan watched them moving slowly, and tiredly; their rifles in their limp hands.

"What are you going to do?" asked Katherine quietly.

Morgan turned. Katherine was seated at the kitchen table, staring at nothing. He could barely make out her weary, drawn face in the dim light of the candle there.

"I wish I knew," answered Morgan. "We've taken the risk and its turned against us." He smiled sadly. "Did I think I was going to be a hero in all this?"

"I never thought the children would have to die," Katherine said, her voice breaking, and tears streaming down her face.

Morgan looked away to the empty street, and the long rows of dimly lighted houses. It all looked unreal—like a dull, faded oil painting in colors of gray and black, and deep blue. There were no sounds any more from any of the houses.

"Maybe we should have stayed put," said Morgan, almost to himself, "accepted what we had, what we were; instead of gambling it all for what we hoped; what we thought we deserved."

"And if we do win," said Katherine, "will it have been worth the cost? Will what we lost ever be regained?"

Morgan walked out, letting the screen door close quietly behind him. He started slowly up the center of the main street, not feeling the ground under him or the cool breeze against his hot, unshaven face. His arms hung limply at his sides. His eyes began glancing to the shattered windows of the houses on his right and left. He saw men moving around inside, sometimes women, sometimes children; all sad-faced. Some were weeping—even the men. But the people seemed far away to him, as if he were seeing them through the foggy lens of a long spyglass. But he was able to feel their torment, their anxiety. He knew the names behind all the faces, yet it seemed like he was seeing the faces for the first time. He wanted to save them, but no longer knew how. The heart went out of him, along with his courage and hope. He stood at the far end of the long street for a time; the houses on both sides fading slightly, and the light from the broken windows casting a soft, fuzzy glow. The dark street began stretching away, on and on, disappearing into a black wall.

CHAPTER 12

By eight o'clock the next morning, the sun beat down with an oven-like heat. Morgan stood once again in the middle of the main street. His haggard, whisker-covered face showing the effects of a night without sleep; a night of unending thoughts. Setting before him was a battered metal washtub on top an equally battered wooden crate. Tom Mitchell stood beside him, stone-faced, and looking just as exhausted as Morgan. Both men were unarmed. Behind them stood Katherine McAlister. Despite the heat of the day, she clutched a thin shawl around her shoulders, as if to protect herself from a growing chill.

Morgan McAlister and Tom Mitchell said nothing as a long line of men and women moved silently towards them. From the porches, from behind broken screen doors and broken windows, the children watched; many of them with their thin, bare arms around each other.

Without a look or a word, the men and women dropped a small scrap of paper into the battered washtub. An "X" on the paper was the sign for fighting on; a blank scrap, for ending the strike; accepting whatever Chase and Harwick chose to give them—even if it meant packing up and leaving.

After dropping their scraps of paper into the tub, the men and women walked away to their homes. But one woman, tall, and heavy-boned, wearing a thin, ragged dress, flung her scrap of paper in Morgan's face. She stood looking at him with all the hate that was in her.

"My sweet baby boy is dead. And his sweet baby sister," said the woman, tears coming to her eyes. "Tell us again what a great and wonderful thing this strike will be."

Morgan could only close his eyes in response.

"You've taken my life away with your empty words."

"Rachel, please," said Katherine, and held out a hand to her.

"I don't want sympathy. I want my babies."

"Woman," said Tom Mitchell, sternly, forcing himself to look the woman in the face, "you're not the only one who's had a loss. Move on."

"I'll move," replied the woman, as she walked on past, "and curse you till the day you die."

"They're coming," shouted a man standing on the roof of one of the nearby houses.

Everyone glanced to him, then towards the Breakers' camp.

"I see trucks!" shouted another man from the roof of a house further up the street. "Lots of trucks, on the main road!"

"Well," said Mitchell, "so much for voting. I guess the decision's been made for us."

"Get to your places," shouted Kelly Pike, standing on top an overturned coal wagon, waving his rifle in the air. "Hurry up, move!"

Most of the men began running to their assigned positions at the barricades, but some remained where they were, glancing at each other, unsure of what to do; unsure if they had the strength to go on. The women, however, began running back to the houses to protect the children.

By the time Morgan McAlister and Tom Mitchell had joined the others at the barricades they had their rifles, and only five extra cartridges in their pockets. They stared into the distance at the main road leading into the housing area. A long line of trucks appeared, the road dust boiling in all around them like a hazy curtain. The Breakers could be seen moving agitatedly through the whole camp—pointing and watching the trucks.

Morgan wiped the sweat from his face and checked his rifle, even though the overwhelming show of force coming towards them could not be defeated.

"God," said Mitchell to himself, "how many more did they bring in?" He flicked the safety of his rifle to "off", and raised it to his shoulder.

Morgan climbed to the top of the barricade and stood there.

"What are you doing?" gasped Mitchell. "Get the hell down!"

Nearby, other men yelled for Morgan to get off the barricade. He ignored them. Mitchell grabbed at Morgan's pant leg, but Morgan jerked free.

"Come down, man," shouted Mitchell. "You want to die?"

Morgan looked down, expressionless. "I started this. Let me finish it."

Mitchell made another grab at Morgan, but he dodged it and jumped down on the other side of the barricade. He walked a few yards along the road and stopped, his rifle cradled casually across his left arm.

The thirty large trucks increased their speed, and the noisy line came rattling closer. Suddenly some of them turned into the center of the Breakers' camp, while the rest proceeded up the road towards mine seven.

Inside the Breakers' camp, the milling groups of men stood dumbfounded, as armed soldiers, of the National Guard, began jumping from the now slow-moving trucks. Several of the trucks pulled out of line and stopped. More soldiers jumped off and began setting up water-cooled, thirty caliber machine guns. More machine-gun crews scrambled to the tops of the boxcars, and within minutes the muzzels of their weapons were sweeping back and forth above the stunned mob.

Morgan McAlister stood calmly in the center of the road, watching the lead truck drive towards him. It stopped only a few yards away. From the trucks at the rear, more helmeted soldiers began deploying; the long, sharp bayonets attached to their rifles gleamed in the sunlight. They rushed in a line to the right and left of the main road, and stood facing the housing area of the miners. They pulled the bolts back on their rifles, then jammed them forward, shoving a cartridge into the breach. They stood at port-arms, ready to aim and fire.

From the lead truck an officer climbed down from the passenger side, the gold leafs of his Major's insignia shining bright on the top of his shoulders. He was dressed in dark khaki, but wore highly polished brown riding boots. There was a holster, and forty-five caliber Colt automatic pistol buckled tightly around his protruding belly. His steel helmet was strapped tightly to his head, causing the cheeks of his pasty white face to bulge outward as if made of dough. He forced his squatted frame upright, making himself as tall as he could. He walked towards Morgan, hoping the hard stare of his dull gray eyes would intimidate him. He came to a stop a few feet from Morgan, glanced him up and down, and began tapping his long leather boots with his swagger stick.

"My name is Major Pennell." His voice was cold and arrogant. "Governor Hallgren has sent me here to end this strike. I have four hundred soldiers, and fourteen machine guns. This situation is now over, and entirely in my control. This is martial law. And if you don't know what that means, I will teach it to you very quickly."

"What about the Breakers," asked Morgan, "are they under martial law?"

"You will not question me, I will question you," replied Pennell loudly. "Remove those barricades."

"Do you give me your word you'll protect these people here?" said Morgan.

"I don't have to give you agitating, Red, striking bastards anything, except bullets."

Pennell turned and walked back to his truck, yelling, "Sergeant!"

"Yes, sir," answered a hulking, burly soldier with a forty-five automatic in his hand.

"Prepare to fire!"

"Yes, sir! Aim!" shouted the sergeant.

Pennell turned and stared at Morgan. Morgan let his rifle fall to the ground, and started back to the barricades. "Open up," he ordered.

Tom Mitchell and the others began dismantling the jumble of lumber and overturned coal wagons. Pennell smiled contemptuously and climbed back into his truck. Morgan stepped to the side of the road, and stood watching as the line of trucks moved into the housing area. Within minutes, the roiling clouds of dust shrouded him, and he faded from view.

The miners were quickly disarmed, and their rifles dumped in random piles, as squads of sharp-eyed soldiers stood watching. Other groups of soldiers hurriedly began pitching tents wherever space was available.

Major Pennell's tent was situated near the mine office, to let everyone know he had been victorious; had accomplished his mission. A large American flag snapped in the wind beside his tent, and a machine-gun had been set up nearby.

In the Breakers' camp, the National Guardsmen had pitched more tents in a large circle around the outer edges of the camp. The city of canvas seemed to go on forever in all directions. Intimidating squads of soldiers moved constantly among the subdued Breakers, disarming them as the miners had been. Otis Garlow, and Bully Boy, remained out of sight, in their tents, peeking through the closed front flaps to see if any soldiers were searching for them.

Hildscheimer, however, and his delicate yellow daffodils, were enjoying the attention of the younger Guardsmen. The smiles and teasing words of the musical ladies were not wasted on the appreciative audience—until an old, growling sergeant stormed in, scattering soldiers, and yellow daffodils, and a protesting Hildscheimer, in different directions.

The sun began to settle in a blinding white ball behind mine seven, but its oppressive heat remained. The floury dust covering the main street blossomed into the air as Sheriff Deets and three car-loads of deputies raced in. The cars squealed to a stop in front of Morgan McAlister's house. Shotgun waving deputies swarmed around the tiny structure, guns aimed at every window and door. Deets, a revolver in one hand, and a warrant in the other, walked boldly up the wooden walk to the front porch.

"McAlister," shouted Deets from the foot of the steps. "This is the law! I got a warrant for your arrest!"

Deets and the deputies waited tensely, but there was no reply from the house; only silence.

"What do you think you're doing?" said a chilling voice from behind Deets.

Deets turned and saw Major Pennell standing in the middle of the street with four armed soldiers. Pennell was tapping his shiny boot with his swagger stick.

"I asked you a question," said Pennell.

Deets walked towards Pennell, waving the warrant. "I'm sheriff Deets; just here to pick up a few people and…"

"If I say you can," interrupted Pennell, snatching the warrant from Deets. "Martial law has been declared," he added, glancing at the warrant.

"I know, but I need…"

"A warrant here is only good if I say it is." Pennell tossed the warrant back to Deets. "Whom do you want?"

"Morgan McAlister to start with. Then Tom Mitchell, Dan Ketchum, Kelly Pike. And I got lots of John Doe warrants for…"

"Dan Ketchum is dead. I've confirmed that. As for the others, they can't be found."

"You sure?" said Deets angrily.

"You think I'm an idiot," said Pennell loudly. "What did I just say?"

"I just…just thought maybe…"

"I assume you're here on behalf of Mr. Chase?"

"Yes, his orders."

"And I'm here on orders from the Governor of Ohio."

"Yeah, sure, but I'm in a tight spot just now, soldier boy, and…"

"Major Pennell, to you."

"Okay, Major, but I need to serve these warrants."

"If I find these men you can have them. I could care less about them."

"That's good. Mind if me and my men nose around? See what we can find."

Pennell's scornful glance swept over the shabby, unshaven deputies, then back to Deets. "Help yourself," he replied, then pointed his swagger stick at Deets. "But before you do a thing here, it will require my permission. Or you'll be the one under arrest. Understood?"

"Whatever you say, Major."

Pennell turned sharply and proceeded up the street, followed by his armed escort.

Deets watched contemptuously, then spit. "Strutting peacock son-of-a-bitch," he said quietly.

Even though the sun had set hours ago, all the rooms in Booth McAlister's house were dark, except for the electric ceiling light in the kitchen. Hope McAlister sat at the small table there, silently eating her dinner of boiled potatoes and corned beef. After taking a small bite she set her knife and fork down. Her hard, dark eyes turned to the empty living room. She rose slowly, took a cane in each hand and moved out of the kitchen, across the living room, and down the narrow hallway to her bedroom door. She stopped and looked across the way to the closed door of Booth's bedroom, and listened. She could hear muffled voices.

Morgan McAlister was pacing agitatedly from one side of the small room to the other. Tom Mitchell sat on the edge of the bed, wiping his sweating face with a dirty red handkerchief. Booth stood in one corner, anxiously watching Morgan. Katherine McAlister was beside an open window, its two curtain panels pulled together creating a narrow slit in the center to look through.

"This is all wrong," said Morgan angrily. "I should be out there with those men."

"It won't do any good," replied Booth. "You're only chance now is to get away. You and Tom."

"I heard that's what Kelly Pike done," said Mitchell. "Soon as the Guard come in, he lit out, saying they'd never arrest him, or put him in jail, for doing what was right."

Morgan stopped his pacing and looked at Mitchell. "What good's it going to do to run?"

"At least it gives you a chance to go on," said Booth.

"Go on to what?" asked Morgan.

"To continue what you started," said Booth.

"It's over; it's dead," replied Morgan, and began pacing again.

"I don't think it is," said Booth. "When Chase called me, and said Deets and his deputies were on the way, and to keep an eye on you and Tom, he sounded worried. Chase wants you two; wants to shut you up."

"Permanently?" asked Mitchell.

"Maybe," answered Booth. "Chase even told me he'll let truck loads of food supplies in once you and Tom are under arrest."

"What a generous man," said Mitchell.

"You shouldn't be getting involved with us, Booth," said Morgan.

Booth looked down for a moment, then spoke. "Yes, I should. I stood by, in the beginning, but I should have done something to help you." He looked at Morgan. "I'm not going to turn away this time, not after all those men, women, and children have died."

"There are men coming," said Katherine softly, staring through a slit in the curtains. Morgan and the others looked to her and waited. "Deputies," she whispered.

Three deputies came along the wooden sidewalk to the entrance gate of Booth's house and stopped. They studied the dark house a moment then went on. Katherine turned from the window.

"I agree with Booth," she said. "Letting Deets take you and Tom will do nothing; prove nothing."

"We can't hide forever," said Morgan.

"Just for a few days," said Booth. "Maybe not that long."

"Then what?" asked Mitchell.

"I'll take you both out of here," replied Booth.

"How?" asked Katherine, anxiously.

"As superintendent, I'll be able to move in and out of here pretty much as I please. The Guardsmen will be watching the miners, and the Breakers."

"But Morgan and Tom have to go soon," said Katherine. "What if the soldiers begin searching the houses, and the mine?"

"I know," said Booth, "we don't have much time. But I'll think of something. We have to find a lawyer who will take your case; and have the nerve to stand up against Chase and Harwick."

"We don't have money for that," said Mitchell in disgust, and got up.

"You're only chance of surviving this to go to court," said Booth. "Let the whole world know what this was all about. If Chase ends it here, you're finished. All these people are finished."

"What do we have to do?" asked Katherine.

"For now, Morgan and Tom will stay here," said Booth. "There's a small attic at the end of the house. Katherine, you'll have to keep away from here, if Deets and his men see you coming in and out, they could get curious."

"And don't tell my family nothing," added Mitchell. "Those kids of mine can't keep a secret to save their souls."

Katherine came up behind Morgan and put her arms around him. "It's the only way," she whispered. "If we can do this, there's still a chance of winning something."

Booth and Mitchell stared at Morgan till he finally turned to them. A calm, determined expression was on his face. "Let's do it," he said. "And let Chase and Harwick roast in Hell."

As Booth and the others continued making their plans, Hope stood just outside the door listening.

———————

The mood at the Breakers' camp was dreary and grim. The men had been stripped of their guns and ammunition, and now sat around their campfires eating their evening meal, talking in low voices, and watching the squads of armed soliders stroll back and forth across the sprawling camp. The concerts of the all-girl orchestra had been outlawed, and the "yellow daffodils" ordered to remain in their tents or be arrested. Hildscheimer had raised a loud protest to Major Pennell, and was promptly locked inside one of the boxcars so he wouldn't miss the first train out.

As for Gentleman Jim, Handsome, and Oracle, they stayed to themselves at their brush protected campsite. Whenever a detail of armed soldiers came past, the three would simply smile and nod, and act as meek as children. But an hour before curfew, Handsome said he wanted to walk about the camp; listen to what the Breakers were saying; what the soldiers were saying.

Jim and Oracle sat cross-legged near their small fire, finishing their plate of soggy beans, and fatty chunks of ham.

"Why didn't Handsome finish eating?" asked Oracle.

"Don't know," replied Jim, looking in the direction Handsome had gone. "He doesn't seem to be himself tonight."

"This is my favorite," said Oracle, banging his spoon on the edge of his tin plate. "Pig is good."

"You must have a caste iron stomach," said Jim, and emptied his plate onto Oracle's.

"I don't think so," said Oracle, thinking about it, then began spooning the greasy ham and beans into his mouth.

The two turned quickly when they heard someone approaching through the waist-high brush behind them. It was Handsome.

Handsome squatted at the fire before he spoke. "Word's going round we're all going to be put on a train and hauled back to Chicago and dumped."

"Yes," said Jim, "when I saw all those bright, shiny bayonets, I had a premonition our prospects here were at an end."

"Fine with me," said Handsome, and crawled into the small tent he shared with Jim and Oracle. He began rummaging around.

Jim watched, then said, "Handsome, before we vacate the premises, I'd like you to help me do one more little thing—if we can get by the soldiers."

"No, Jim," said Oracle, deeply worried. "If we leave the camp we'll be shot dead. The soldiers said so."

Handsome laughed as he came out of the tent and stood up. His blanket was rolled up and under his arm, and tied tightly at both ends with thick twine. "Those sentries would need eyes like a cat to hit anything this time of night."

"What are you doing, Handsome?" asked Jim.

"Like you said, our prospects here are at an end. Time to move on."

Jim got to his feet, studied Handsome a moment. "I had plans for the three of us to leave together."

"You forgot about the pretty little thing that lives over the way there," he said with a smile.

"Made her a glowing promise, did you?" said Jim.

"Can't back out now."

"I was hoping you'd gotten that out of your system."

"You haven't seen her, Jim."

Jim looked at Oracle. "See what love does to people?"

"But you love us, don't you, Handsome?" said Oracle.

"You and Jim will do just fine without me," said Handsome. He held out his hand to Jim. "Good luck, pardner."

Jim's face darkened. His eyes seemed to grow large and wild-looking. He stared at Handsome without taking his hand. "We made a pledge, the three of us," he said. "Did you forget?" His voice was calm, but touched with a dangerous edge.

"That's right," said Oracle, dropping his plate, and getting to his knees. He took hold of Handsome's coattail. "When...when we were in...you know, that place. We swore a pledge."

"Yes," said Jim. "To stay together; be loyal. Loyalty above all."

"Please don't go," said Oracle, tears glistening in his big sad eyes. "You're one of us. You promised to take care of me."

"Jim can do that better than me, Oracle."

"You're letting us down, Handsome," said Jim.

"I'm tired of this life," said Handsome. "Ain't you? Don't you ever dream of something different?"

"Of course," said Jim. "I dream..." he stopped himself and turned his eyes to the fire, embarrassed that he had dropped his façade.

"What?" asked Handsome, coming closer. "Tell me."

Jim looked at Handsome and smiled weakly. "My books," he said gently. "A long, long time ago, I could hide away in the silence of a room, and just read and read. Surrounded by all those wonderful, magnificent friends. Reading about a world that was young and unfouled. Adventures in paradise." Suddenly his expression grew hostile. "Just dreams that would never come true. Dead at birth." He turned to Oracle. "And what's your dream? What is it you want the most?"

Oracle grinned. "An ice cream cone."

"Why?"

"I never had one."

"Very profound, Oracle."

"I got to git," said Handsome, holding out his hand again.

Again, Jim refused to take it, and spoke to Oracle. "What say you? Should we let our friend go?"

Oracle stared at Handsome, then Jim. Tears streaked his cheeks. "It breaks my heart. But why give a bird wings if you won't let him fly?"

Jim nodded tiredly, and held out his hand to Handsome. They gripped hands tightly. "At times I wonder if God really created us," said Jim.

"What?" said Handsome, puzzled. "Why?"

"Because there's so much Devil in us."

Handsome shook his head. "Now you're talking way past me. You should have been a lawyer."

"What's a lawyer?" asked Oracle, wiping his eyes and getting to his feet, very interested in this new word.

"A lawyer," said Jim, "is someone who makes people like us look good."

"Oh," said Oracle, thoughtfully, and concentrated on what Jim had told him.

"Even Christ cursed the lawyers," added Jim. "Tells you a lot, doesn't it?"

"I got to go," said Handsome, and turned quickly away.

"Wait," said Jim. He crossed to Handsome and entwined his left arm around Handsome's right arm. "Let me walk a way with you; see you off safely."

Handsome glanced back and winked at Oracle. "Good luck, pardner. Hope you get that ice cream cone."

"Don't go," whispered Oracle. "Don't go into the darkness."

As Jim and Handsome walked away, Jim spoke in a gentle, fatherly tone. "One last piece of advice, Handsome. The world's a vicious wolf; don't turn your back on it."

Seconds later, Oracle lost sight of them. He put his hands to his face, and covered his eyes.

The tall, ornate grandfather clock in Brewster Harwick's study sounded a heavy gong-like tone—the rhythm of a funeral march almost. Its monotonous midnight droning filled the huge room. Brewster was seated at an elaborately hand-carved mahogany desk, a telephone receiver to his ear, and a fat, smoldering cigar clamped between his teeth. He wore a pair of loose fitting black silk pajamas, and a black silk robe and slippers. The small desk lamp cast a circle of light on Brewster and part of the desk, leaving the rest of the room dark.

"And I expect you here, early in the morning," Brewster said into the phone. "Don't worry about having breakfast, you can eat later." He listened for a few seconds to Addison Chase's voice then interrupted. "I don't care," he shouted. "That son-of-a-bitch Hallgren had no right to send in the National Guard! I want you to call him and tell that worthless gutter rat to call me and explain why he did it."—"Don't give me any excuses! Do what I tell you, or do you think you're in control here?"—"What do you mean, we're done?" The telephone line went dead. Brewster clicked the receiver cradle frantically, then grabbed the telephone and hurled it against the wall. "You think you can hang up on me?" he shouted. "You worthless, weak-kneed, bastard!"

Bright lights flashed across the open windows of the study, and an automobile could be heard stopping at the steps of the front porch. Brewster crossed quickly to the windows and leaned out. He saw his Packard limousine, with its engine idling, and his uniformed chauffeur holding open the rear passenger door. Brewster's two young daughters, dressed in hat and coat, ran down the front steps and into the limousine. Abigail followed, also in hat and coat. Two of her personal maids came next, each with two suitcases. The chauffeur helped them place the suitcases in the trunk and closed the lid.

"What are you doing?" shouted Brewster.

Startled, the maids hurried back into the house. The chauffeur remained at the rear of the limousine, unsure of what to do or say. But Abigail, calm and confident, took a few steps in Brewster's direction and waved.

"You should go to bed, Brewster," she said. "Get so rest. You're going to need it."

"What the hell are you doing?"

"What the hell does it look like? You can ship the rest of my things to me. I'm returning to Chicago."

"And I say you're not!"

Abigail gave a short laugh. "I hope you have a good attorney, Brewster."

"Attorney?"

"Yes, I'll be getting a divorce. Among other things."

"Divorce? Fine! And you'll end up in the gutter where you belong."

"You're the one who should be worrying about that," replied Abigail coolly. "Goodbye you son-of-a-bitch."

"Whore," shouted Brewster, and threw his cigar in her direction. "You always were, and you always will be!"

Abigail turned to the chauffeur. "Drive." She stepped into the rear of the limousine, the chauffeur closed the door, and got behind the wheel.

Brewster stormed out of the study, through the entrance hall, and out onto the front porch. He began shouting threats and obscenities, and his hoarse, raging voice revealed the contempt and disgust he harbored for the woman he never loved, and for the two daughters he never wanted. As the taillights of the limousine disappeared down the long driveway, Brewster returned to the house, slamming the door with all his might. His eyes were crazed, and his face savage and red. He glanced around the dark entrance hall like a trapped animal. Grabbing a tall, brass coat rack, near the door, he flung in through the stained glass panels of the door. Next he picked up a three foot tall, ceramic umbrella stand, raised it over his head and smashed it against the floor.

"You think you can leave me?" he shouted. "You think you can threaten me? I'll destroy you!"

He stumbled up the long staircase towards the second floor, his silk robe open and streaming out behind him like a cape. Sweat was streaming down his face, and his rage made his vision blurry. Halfway up the stairs he stopped abruptly, and stood staring. In the deep shadows at the top of the stairs something moved. As Brewster's breathing eased, he saw a figure—short and crouched—like one of those gargoyles that are perched at the eaves of a towering cathedral. After a moment, the black lump stood up.

"Things not going as planned, Mr. Harwick?" asked Gentleman Jim.

"Get out my house you filthy scum," snarled Brewster, and rushed on into his brightly lighted bedroom.

Jim followed calmly.

Brewster stood at an open window on the far side of the bedroom, staring out. There was no sign of the limousine's headlights or taillights.

"I was always of the opinion people shouldn't expect too much of one another," said Jim, leaning in the doorway.

Brewster turned, glaring at Jim. "If you came for more money, you'll rot before you get it."

"No, no, no," replied Jim in a friendly voice. "The arrival of the National Guard has definitely put an end to all my plans. I just stopped by to say farewell."

"Get out," said Brewster, and turned back to the open window.

"I don't know why people are surprised when someone treats them badly," said Jim.

Brewster rushed towards the night table beside his bed then stopped. The drawer was pulled halfway out. Brewster looked at Jim, who just shrugged.

"Money has always been my greatest weakness," said Jim.

Brewster jerked open the drawer further. All the stacks of tightly bound money were gone, but the small, shiny revolver was still there.

"I'll see you rot in prison, you little thieving…"

"I'm afraid I've already done that," said Jim, with a smile. "Didn't care much for it."

Brewster took the revolver from the drawer, and pointed it at Jim.

"One last question, Mr. Harwick," said Jim, holding up a finger. "You've had the opportunity to become ruthlessly rich, while I've had the opportunity to become ruthlessly evil. But…which one of us is the more depraved?"

Brewster took a step forward and pulled the trigger. There was only a click. He pulled the trigger again and again.

Jim put both hands in his coat pocket and came close to Brewster. His drew his left fist from his pocket, and when he opened it six small cartridges fell to the carpet.

"Do you hear the harps of heaven, Mr. Harwick?" asked Jim, menacingly. "Or is that the Devil's fiddle?"

Brewster lunged at Jim, trying to strike him across the head with the revolver, but Jim was quicker. His right hand shot from his coat pocket, and with a flick of his wrist, he snapped open the long blade of his pocket knife.

The two men stood nose to nose. Brewster let out a surprised grunt, and took a few steps back. A look of shock and amazement filled his eyes and face. The razor-sharp blade had created a gnawing sting, then a hard throbbing in his chest. He looked down. Blood was soaking through the black silk of his pajama tops. He staggered slightly, and dropped to his knees beside the bed. He stared at Jim, tried to raise the revolver, but was too weak.

Jim shook his head. "Sad," he said softly. "There doesn't seem to be any values to live by any more. You can get by with anything if you know how to play the game, Mr. Harwick."

Brewster began to choke and gurgle. Blood was dripping from his nose and mouth.

"Have to go," said Jim cheerfully. "It's way past my curfew." He politely tipped his dirty, stained cap and left the room, closing the door quietly.

CHAPTER 13

The morning sky was turning a pearl gray, and the black silhouettes of the surrounding hills, with their stunned trees and jagged rocks, were just beginning to reveal their stark shapes. A shrill scream shattered the stillness. The warning whistle of mine seven was telling the miners they had fifteen minutes to be at their jobs.

Without a word to one another, the miners filed along the main street towards the mine, their half-empty lunch pails dangling from their hands. Their blank expressions and hollowed-eyed stares made their faces as lifeless and hard as the coal they were going to dig out of the deep dark tunnels.

The women and children stood on the narrow porches watching the slow march of the men—their faces, too, just as expressionless and hollow-eyed.

The only thing that hadn't changed was the mine itself. All the grimy, drab buildings, the coal breakers, the coal wagons, and the criss-crossed sections of the steel railroad tracks remained as impersonal and solid as the mountain behind it. The tall chimneys of the boiler house billowed towering clouds of smoke into the slowly brightening sky. The men were returning to their twelve hour workday—seven days a week—to make up for the losses suffered by Harwick Coal Company during the strike. But all that mattered now was survival—it was work or starve.

Addison Chase had again sent word to Booth McAlister that no miner would be fired or removed from his home; he wanted to be fair about things; he admired the honest workingman. But as for Morgan McAlister and Tom Mitchell, they were not included in his message of forgiveness and admiration. They were outcasts, and were to be punished.

Hope McAlister sat on the front porch in her rocking chair, rocking back and forth, her piercing dark eyes watching the horizon. A heavy wool shawl was wrapped around her, her two canes lying beside her chair. She had been sitting there long before the warning whistle had sounded. Soldiers stood at intervals along the entire length of the main street, their rifles at their sides, with the sharp-edged bayonets pointing up. The miners walked by without a glance at them.

Hope stopped her rocking when she heard movement inside the house, then the soft voices of men. She heard footsteps crossing the living room to the kitchen; then the hurried footsteps of one man as he came to the screen door of the porch.

"We're going," said Booth, in a tense voice. "If Katherine comes, tell her I'll see her when I get back."

Hope said nothing, and began rocking again.

"Hope?" said Booth in a worried tone.

"I heard you," said Hope, coldly.

When Booth started back towards the kitchen, Hope took a cane in each hand, and struggled out of the rocker. She started slowly down the steps of the porch.

Booth stepped out of the back door of the kitchen, leaving it open. He glanced to his right and left then walked quickly to his small pickup truck parked a few yards away. After taking another quick look around, he motioned subtly with one hand. Morgan McAlister and Tom Mitchell came out of the house and climbed into the rear of the pickup. Booth threw a heavy canvas tarp over them, then went to the opposite side of the truck, grabbed two long pieces of rusty, corrugated tin roofing, and placed them on top the canvas. Next came small, empty wooden boxes till the truck was filled end to end.

Hope came ambling along the wooden sidewalk of the main street, her eyes on Major Pennell, standing with his back to her. He was pointing one way then another with his swagger stick, issuing his orders of the day to a detail of armed soldiers.

"Excuse me," said Hope.

Pennell turned his head and glanced her up and down. "I'm very busy at the moment," he said roughly and turned away.

"Too busy to do your job?" asked Hope.

Pennell turned completely around, his mouth open slightly in surprise, and he just stared.

Booth drove his pickup truck around to the front of his house and stopped. He could see armed soldiers moving along both sides of the street. Here and there, women were beginning to come out of the houses, going next door or across the street to a neighboring house, hoping to borrow a little flour, a little salt or lard, if any were to be had.

Booth shifted the truck into second gear and proceeded along the street, he wanted to sped up, but forced himself to remain calm. It was then he noticed Hope walking up the sidewalk, back towards their house. Her gaze was on the ends of her two canes, then, when she heard Booth's truck, she looked up. Their eyes met briefly—Hope's cold and distant; Booth's squinting with uncertainty and foreboding. He kept watching her as she walked on. Suddenly a National Guard truck roared out of an alley from between two of the houses, blocking the main street. Four soldiers stood in the bed of the open truck, leaning against the waist-high railing, their rifles aimed directly at Booth. He stopped his truck quickly. Four more soldiers rushed out of a house to his right, aiming their rifles at him. Booth raised his hands and sat perfectly still. Major Pennell walked up from the rear of the truck, slapping the driver's door hard with his swagger stick. Booth couldn't help flinching.

"Turn that engine off," said Pennell.

"What's wrong, Major?" asked Booth, doing as told. "You gave me a pass to go into Palmyra, remember?"

"Get out," shouted Pennell, slapping the windshield savagely with his swagger stick.

"I don't understand," said Booth, getting out.

"You will. Put your hands on top your head, and don't move."

Pennell motioned to the four soldiers on the far side of the truck. They began throwing the small wooden boxes from the back. When the canvas tarp was pulled up, Morgan McAlister and Tom Mitchell lay squinting into the bright morning sun.

"Out," shouted Pennell. "Get out!"

The two men climbed out, and stood facing Pennell. Mitchell smirked, and a slight smile grew on Morgan's face as they looked at the short, puffy imitation soldier in front of them. Their attitudes only increased Pennell's hostility and scorn.

"McAlister and Mitchell, I assume?" said Pennell.

"And what's your name, tin soldier?" asked Mitchell.

Pennell raised his swagger stick to strike, but Morgan stepped in front of Mitchell, saying, "We're unarmed, and your prisoners, Major, but we still have rights here."

"Rights?" screamed Pennell. "You rabble scum! You Red, unionizing, agitating muck!"

"Go to National Guard Hell," said Mitchell, and spit on Pennell's shiny boots.

Pennell swung his swagger stick at Mitchell, but Morgan snatched it away, snapped it in two, and flung it to the ground. Pennell's eyes looked as if they were going to pop from their sockets.

"These men don't deserve to be treated like criminals," said Booth, stepping forward.

"Is that so?" shouted Pennell. "And what the hell do you think's going to happen to you!"

"It doesn't matter. But every man here—every woman and child here—deserves to be heard concerning what went on here. You don't know what..."

"And I don't care! The governor sent me to deal with you scum, and that's exactly what I'll do."

"I'm the superintendent of this mine, and..."

"Not any more. Corporal," shouted Pennell.

A corporal ran up quickly and came to attention. "Yes, sir?"

"You will take these three into Palmyra. Turn them over to Sheriff Deets; he has arrest warrants on two of them."

"Yes, sir."

Pennell's eyes moved from Morgan to Mitchell as he said, "I'm sure Deets has something special planned for you, after all the murder and mayhem you've caused."

"Morgan!"

Everyone turned and saw Katherine McAlister running up the street towards them.

"Go home, Katherine," yelled Morgan. "There's nothing you can do."

"Stop her," ordered Pennell loudly.

Two soldiers stepped forward, grabbing Katherine by the arms.

"Leave her alone," shouted Morgan.

Pennell whirled around and shoved Morgan violently against Booth's truck. "Get him out of here," screamed Pennell. "Get them all out of here!"

The soldiers began herding Booth, Morgan, and Mitchell to the large open truck blocking the main street. Pennell, flustered and humiliated by the defiance to his authority, stooped down and snatched up his mangled swagger stick. He tried to force it back together, but it was useless. He saw the women and children staring at him from the porches and windows, and he began pointing at them.

"Yes," he shouted. "Look! Look! You defy me and you'll regret it! Every one of you!"

The women and children rushed from the porches, and the faces at the shattered windows disappeared.

The National Guard truck drove away with Booth, Morgan, and Mitchell, in the rear, leaning against the cab, and six armed soldiers a few feet from them, watching them. Katherine was running behind the truck, it dusty wake flowing over her. The truck increased its speed, and Katherine tried to keep up until two women ran into the street and stopped her. They remained there as the truck became smaller and smaller.

————————

The harsh whistle of the large locomotive kept up a constant piercing scream as it steamed slowly backward along the tracks to the long line of boxcars at the edge of the Breakers' camp—a camp that was rapidly disappearing. All the tents had been pulled down, rolled up, and piled in heaps, like miniature hay stacks. Rifles and handguns were piled high on spread blankets; cartridges of all calibers had been deposited in buckets and cooking pots in the center of the huge camp. Despite the patrols of armed soldiers, and sheriff's deputies, the Breakers were relaxed—happy. They had received their final pay—in cash—and were about to be given a free train ride back to Chicago. When ordered to board the train, the men promptly obeyed, laughing and joking.

Gentleman Jim sat with his back resting against a rotted log, carefully cleaning his fingernails with the point of his pocket knife. Every so often he would glance at the chaotic movements of the soldiers and Breakers milling around the waiting train. Clouds of powdery dust drifted high in the air, engulfing the men in a dirty haze. Jim's attention then turned to Sheriff Deets and a deputy, who came walking towards him, revolvers drawn.

"The picnic's over, bindle-stiff," said Deets. "On your feet."

Jim smiled and put his knife away as he stood up. "Thank you, sheriff, I wouldn't want to miss my train."

A large touring car, driven by a scruffy-looking deputy, came to a stop a few yards away. "Sheriff," yelled the deputy, "McAlister and Mitchell have been caught."

"You sure?" said Deets rushing towards the car.

The deputy pointed into the distance. "They're in that National Guard truck, and headed for Palmyra. They arrested Booth McAlister too."

"Hot damn," said Deets, smiling, and scrambled into the front passenger seat. "I'm really going to enjoy this."

The other deputy leaped into the rear of the open car, and it sped off through the camp, raising a tall rooster tail of thick dust. Jim stood calmly, watching it try to catch up to the National Guard truck.

"Strange, the sort of people who serve the law," said Jim to himself.

"Jim! Jim!"

Jim looked to the sound of Oracle's frantic voice. Oracle came running up, tears streaming down his face.

"Oracle, what is it?"

"Handsome," said Oracle, sobbing and dropping to his knees. "He's dead, Jim."

"What?" replied Jim, giving the impression of being shocked. "No."

"Yes," cried Oracle. "I told him not to go. I told him."

"The miners," said Jim, looking towards the mine. "It had to have been them."

"I'm going to kill all of them," yelled Oracle, springing to his feet. "Every one of them." He started to run.

Jim tackled him and brought him to the ground. "No, no, no," said Jim in a soothing tone. "They'll kill you, just like Handsome. I can't have that. I need you, Oracle. I need you with me."

Oracle grew calm then stared down, sadly. "They cut his throat, Jim," he said weakly. "They...they cut his face all up. I could hardly recognize him."

Jim let go of Oracle and stood up. "Poor Handsome."

Oracle rose quickly and pointed to the center of the camp, where two soldiers, escorted by two armed soldiers, were carrying a body in a thin blanket.

"It's Handsome," whispered Oracle.

Jim took off his cap; Oracle did the same. "God rest his wonderful soul," said Jim.

Oracle looked at Jim. "How long does it take to get a soul?"

"In this world," replied Jim, "probably forever."

"Once," began Oracle, wiping his eyes with his cap, "Handsome said we were broken souls; broken souls that don't have a chance anywhere."

"Yes," said Jim softly, "we just don't seem to fit in, do we?"

"I pray, Jim."

"Why?"

"It makes me feel better."

Jim shrugged. "Why pray when the world belongs to the Devil?"

"You sure?"

"It certainly doesn't belong to us."

"So this is just another place where we don't fit in," said Oracle sadly. "But...I think...if we keep dreaming...we'll find a place; a big bright room with big bright windows. And a soft, soft bed with thick warm blankets to keep us warm at night."

Jim smiled tiredly, put a hand on Oracle's shoulder, and began leading him towards the train. "Time to go," he said. "Destiny is calling."

"I don't hear anything," replied Oracle.

"Listen closely; very closely."

Jim kept his hand on Oracle as they walked; Oracle towering over Jim by more than a foot. The two looked almost comical—a short, thin man leading a bulky, lumbering elephant of a man to catch the circus train.

———————

Only a few days had passed since the Breakers had been taken away. Morgan and Booth McAlister, and Tom Mitchell were still locked away in the Palmyra jail, under constant guard. No visitors allowed. Major Pennell and his soldiers were also gone, as were Sheriff Deets and his deputies. It was as if nothing had ever happened. Work had begun on the new company store and community hall at mine seven—the cost to be deducted from the miners' wages. There were no objections from the men or their families; the only concern now was to keep working, keep food on the table.

The sun flamed to a brilliant red just before sunset, turning the sky dark blue and hazy. A smart-looking, polished Buick coup drove slowly along the main street of the housing area, and the curious eyes of the women and children followed its progress. A few mongrel dogs began trotting along side the auto, barking ineffectual threats, then walking away as if they'd successfully defended their territory. The shiny Buick stopped near three small children, playing with wooden blocks in the powdery dust at the edge of the road. The driver asked for directions, and the children pointed on up the street.

The auto traveled on until it was opposite Morgan McAlister's house. A young, impressive looking man got out. He wore a brown suit, clean white shirt, and dark red tie. His neatly creased fedora hat shaded his tanned face. He walked towards the porch of the house, but before he reached the steps, Katherine McAlister came out, wiping her hands on a thin, damp dish towel.

The young man took off his hat and nodded politely. "Mrs. McAlister?"

Katherine looked him up and down then glanced at the shiny Buick. "You from Harwick Coal?"

The man gave a quick smile. "God forbid. My name is John McKenna."

His smile, and friendly tone eased Katherine's tensions, but she was still wary of him, and what he wanted. The women and children of the surrounding houses were also apprehensive, and kept watching McKenna's every move.

"Your name doesn't tell me much," said Katherine.

"A while back a man named Roscoe Brodie came here," began McKenna. "Wore a straw skimmer, looking like he was getting ready to start dancing in a Hollywood musical."

"I remember him," replied Katherine. "Union man. Gave a big speech, then disappeared."

"You didn't pay him any union dues, did you?"

"With what, coal dust?"

McKenna couldn't help grinning. "Mr. Brodie was a bit of a drinker when he had a pocket of greenbacks. But he was a damn good promoter."

"Why you so interested in him?"

"He works for us."

"Us?"

"Our union."

Katherine smiled tiredly and shook her head.

"Something wrong, ma'am?"

"Well, I'll tell you; the miners here, and their families, wanted a better life, a better future. The Breakers that were camped over there wanted easy money; and they didn't care how they got it. Now you're here, Mr. Union-man, wanting something, too"

"Mr. Brodie first, then..." McKenna gave a quick flick of his eyebrows.

"What?"

"You people may have been defeated. But you're not destroyed."

"Tell that to the men, women, and children up there in the graveyard." Katherine turned to go back inside.

"What happened here wasn't all for nothing," said McKenna. Katherine stopped, but didn't turn to him. "The poor people in that graveyard didn't die for the benefit of Harwick Coal Company. They died so you people, and all the other people, starving and struggling in this world won't have to beg or crawl, or bow down for a lousy nickel raise."

Katherine turned and stared at McKenna.

"Men like your husband," continued McKenna, "and Tom Mitchell, can't give up now. I won't let it happen."

"You?"

"Believe it or not, I used to be a miner. Scratching like a mole, digging blindly in the dark earth. Just a white slave, chiseling out chunks of black diamonds to make the rich richer."

"You're wearing a pretty fancy suit and hat, Mr. Miner," said Katherine, coming to the edge of the porch.

"I've seen the light, as they say. Like your husband did."

"Why you so interested in Morgan?"

"The fight's not over."

"You and this wonderful union of yours coming back with more guns, more men?"

"No, ma'am. We got something better, surer. We got lawyers, just like the rich people do. Out of this struggle something good will be born. It has to be."

"My husband used to talk like that; now where is he?"

"You seen him?"

"I got a better chance of seeing God Almighty."

"Our lawyers can get him out; the others too. But you people have to keep up the fight; cause next time you can win."

"We already fought the good fight. Now we're just tired and beat down. The only change coming is going to be old age and death."

"I disagree," said McKenna, coming closer to the porch. "You got to get the law on your side. Not guns and dynamite. Use the law like the robber barons do. The law this time; not sweat and blood and tears."

McKenna stared up at Katherine, his face and eyes letting her see he believed in what he was saying; that it wasn't just some prepared speech as Roscoe Brodie had given.

Katherine came down two of the porch steps, and stood face to face with him. "And which law are you talking about? The law for the rich, or the law for the poor?"

McKenna smiled at the sarcasm. "I sure like you, Mrs. McAlister, you got a lot of fight in you yet. I'll bet everyone else here does too." He looked towards the mine with its clouds of coal dust and dirt shrouding everything.

Smoke poured from the chimneys of the boiler house, and the deafening crash of the coal breakers could be heard for miles as they tumbled and crushed the chunks of coal and sent them cascading down the long shuts to the holding bins. Two large locomotives, each trailing a mile long line of coal cars behind it steamed and hissed, waiting to be loaded.

"Does look like the entrance to Hell, doesn't it?" said McKenna, turning back to Katherine.

"And you came to save us all from that?"

"You and all the others out there in those coal fields; who want a better life—deserve a better life. So nobody is ever cast off like a sick old dog in the end."

"You know, Mr. McKenna," said Katherine in a friendly tone, "I'm beginning to like you, too."

"Thank you, ma'am."

"Got some coffee on the stove."

"I'd love some."

Katherine started across the porch and McKenna followed. The mine whistle began screaming in long, relentless bursts. McKenna and Katherine looked towards the mine.

"Quittin' time," said Katherine. "Another twelve hours done; another seven dollars and fifty cents earned."